MW00652934

# THE
# VEGETARIAN
# AND
# HER HUNTER

# THE VEGETARIAN AND HER HUNTER

A Novel

Audrey Destin

Comava Press

First Edition

Book design by Audrey Destin

Developmental Editing by Ellie J. Grey

Line Editing by Gail Delaney

Proofreading Editing by Beth Notari

eBook ISBN: 978-1-956734-00-3

Hardcover ISBN: 978-1-956734-01-0

Paperback ISBN: 978-1-956734-02-7

Audiobook ISBN: 978-1-956734-03-4

This book is dedicated to all the women who have been used in any way without consent. Including but not limited to the women who were deceived and persuaded by lies, women who were drugged, women who have been assaulted, and women who have been raped. May you find a moment of peace in these pages. There is nothing wrong with escapism! This book is for you. #MeToo

# Chapter One

## SAMANTHA

*I wasn't always* a vegetarian, but my husband has always been a hunter. Ever since I've known him. Johnny was raised a hunter, and so in a way this is my fault, not his.

My anger, I mean, as I sit here pushing green beans around on my porcelain plate. Glaring at the purple flowers painted in a delicate manner around the edges. Looping and curling.

Purple is supposed to be calming. That's why I

bought these plates. To calm me when we eat together as a family.

Just like the three lavender pillar candles burning in the center of the table. Wax dripping down the sides, the flame casting flickering shadows in the windowless dining room. Fields of yellow flowers and horses grazing, hung in paintings created with warm acrylics brushed by my own hands on the wall.

I painted them to make this room feel like that, with intention. But the smell of charred flesh overpowers the calming aroma the candles produce. The fantasy of harmony in the paintings.

I listen to him chew and I imagine the meat of the deer he shot with his own gun disintegrating into his saliva. I see its dead eyes in my mind, the way they looked when he arrived home with it in his truck. My stomach turns.

He's such a loud a chewer. It's because his lips are so big. They're beautiful and soft against mine, taste like dark coffee usually, but when he eats, they're the bane of me.

Clearly, he wasn't raised to eat quietly like myself. With his mouth closed, breathing through his nose, gently moving the bits of food, and delicately grinding with the molars.

Polite and quiet. That's what my mother always

expected of me. The mother that adopted me. *Chin up, dear. Napkins in the lap, no elbows on the table, and for goodness sakes, close your mouth.*

His mother must have never glared at him the way mine did, out of the corner of her eye, and then directly, whenever I made any sound at all.

No. Whatever he does in there, between his teeth, is disgusting. Violent and loud. And I hate it.

"Johnny. Why are you chewing like that?"

I glare at him across the candlelight. The flames softening the edges of him. He looks up at me, but he doesn't speak, his mouth is full. His eyes are kind though. He's not alarmed nor surprised. He looks almost tired.

I know why he's chewing like that. He always chews like that. He chews like that because he doesn't think to do any different. Because the taste of the animal he's butchered is intoxicating to him. Because he gives in to all his animal whims. And this one says chew like you're trying to prove to every other animal around you that they're next.

"Honestly Johnny, it's disgusting."

I pick up the napkin off my lap, unable to tolerate this rift between us growing any stronger, and throw it onto the table, the candlelight dances like a manic ballerina making a show of the fact that I've now lost my appetite, and maybe my temper. Making it clear that I think it's his fault.

But like I said.

It's not his fault.

It's mine.

I want to be able to fix it, this rift between us. We are family, we shouldn't have this kind of distance at every single meal. But I don't know how to fix it. What can I possibly do?

No matter how much I try, I can't suppress this anger, this canyon that's formed between us. Maybe I feel a kinship with the prey. And that horrifies me, knowing that I am like them, vegetarian, gentle, doe-eyed. That's how I see myself. Doe-eyed. Because that's how other people see me, too.

That's how Dane saw me. When I was fifteen and my mother, the one who adopted me, pulled some strings to get me my first job under the table so I could help *support my family*, and by support our family she meant her *habits*. At that point our family was just her and I. Dane was the man she pulled some strings with. Dane wasn't a good experience in my life. I'm not surprised now, knowing that my mom put a gentle girl in the hands of a hungry man, for work, but it caught me off guard then. Sadly.

The air conditioner is set lower than I like it in the

house, and so I should be cold. But I'm not. I'm hot. Which is unusual because I'm always cold. To please my husband. Because he likes it colder. And I like to please him. So, every room, chair, and couch has blankets because that is a way for us to meet in the middle. We're usually so good at finding the road where we can meet in the middle.

But right now my cheeks and neck are burning hot. The flush penetrates my skin, right down to my bones. I wonder if he sees this. If he can see my temperature rising and just chooses to ignore it, or if I'm the only one in this marriage that it bothers.

I should be over this by now, this basic difference between us. I'm not mad at him for being a man while I'm a woman. I'm not mad at him for working in tech while I stay at home.

I'm not furious that he's a white man in a world run by white men, while I'm a light skinned mixed race girl that knows nothing about where she comes from.

There are a million little differences between Johnny and I so why is it this one thing, him murdering the animals he eats while I eat none at all, that drives me mad?

But it does. It drives me mad. This one thing is our biggest challenge. And I can't explain exactly why, but what I do know is that I desperately want to fix it, and when I think of how to do that, I feel like I've hit a dead end.

I've exhausted my ideas. The candles and the paintings have done nothing to bring us closer in this room. The dining room table feels like the Grand Canyon when it's between us.

I don't want to be mad. I love him, but I've never been good at controlling my anger. It takes a hold of me, and I lose myself to its strength. Its power. I feel it between my teeth first because I clench them, and then between my eyes, in the place it creases. That crease runs deep under my skin, and before I know it, I'm so consumed even my fingers shake.

The chair scratches the wood beneath me as I slide it out, look away from everything between us, and walk past him without making eye contact. I grab the smooth dark wood of the banister, elegance under my fingertips, and walk up the carpeted stairs heavy footed. I'm not stomping, I'm too proud for that, but I'm not, not stomping either.

It won't bother him too much.

We've been married long enough now that he knows I don't really mean anything by any of it. He knows that I don't hate him, I just hate this distance in our moral compasses. I hate that I can't bridge this gap. He knows nothing I just said actually matters. It won't matter when he comes to bed later tonight. I'll still hold him in my arms and lay my head against his chest. I'll fall asleep to the sound of his heartbeat and soft snores. If he wants to, we'll make love. Because our love is stronger than this rift. He knows that if he stays cool, my anger will burn out before dawn. He's the calm to my storm, always, and I love that about him. It's the magic in our relationship.

When people ask the secret to our strong bond, I always say it's the magic.

I don't like that he's a killer. I love animals. I can't eat them. He knows that. And I think in a way he loves that about me. But for some reason it doesn't keep him from killing.

It is barbaric when one thinks about it. An act of nature that goes against our moral compass of not killing, for the sake of survival. Why? Why does he have this drive to kill, and I feel nothing but sick to my stomach when I think about it? The human nature factor frustrates me.

It's torture. In a way. For me. Seeing him like that. As a murderer. Because I love him.

I slam the door behind me and cross our bedroom into the art nook. It's my place to center. To find peace. I pull out my paints and pallet, lay them out carefully, while I study the oil on canvas that I've been working on, a landscape with a dry meadow in the center of a forest. Just looking at it slows my rapid heartbeat.

Only Johnny can make my heart beat like that. With anger or with love. I love Johnny more than any woman has ever loved a man.

Not just because he's thin and strong with stubble on his face that matches the stubble on his head, blondish brown. His stubble is always tight and trimmed like a rugged five o'clock shadow and yes, that turns me on, and maybe that drew me to him, but it's not why I love him. His watery green eyes that feel like I'm looking into a murky lake, one that's hiding something else just beneath the surface, has something to do with it.

I pick up the green and I mix it with a bit of brown, a lake would look good in this painting, maybe that's what I'm missing.

But above everything else, I love his insides.

I love the way he laughs at me with a snicker when I say something witty, without even looking up or making eye contact. I love the way he does look up and make eye contact when he's concerned about something I've said. I know if a joke has gone too far based on the kind of eye contact we share.

His eyes are the windows to his soul, and I can

read them like a book. He knows mine just as well.

That's what it's like being married for as long as we have. Seventeen years. You don't need words. There are no questions about the meaning of specific eye contact. You know each other's soul. And I love almost every inch of Johnny's soul.

Except the murdering inch.

I spread the murky green slowly across an untouched part of the canvas. It's perfect.

I didn't always feel that way about Johnny.

And that's why this anger belongs to me and it's my job to fix it. It showed up in my body, in a place where I used to hide lust. Maybe I was embarrassed of the lust, maybe that's why now there's anger. His murder used to turn me on. I thought it was incredibly hot. Strong. Like muscles rippling over a body in action. I was attracted to the gun in his hand. That's embarrassing to me now.

Embarrassment begets anger sometimes.

It's funny how people change as they grow. It's like when a child loves pink and princesses but then grows into a teenager who dislikes all things girly and only likes books and sophistication.

That's how this thing between Johnny and I happened. This glitch in our relationship.

We met when I was seventeen. Seventeen is still

such a baby. I see that clearly now. So much still undeveloped. Unrefined.

I'd been through so much by then. I was looking for an outlet. For a place to put all my pain. For something to make me feel strong. After what Dane did to me.

It's laughable how grown up I thought I was. I put braids in my curls, lipstick on my mouth, dark eyeliner around my blackened lashes. Placed my small feet in tall heels, let my long brown legs show all the way up to my daisy dukes that barely covered my newly attained curves, and thought that all meant I was grown. But I had so much growing left to do.

Plus, I had major daddy issues. I'd been abandoned by two fathers. I was desperate for adoration by a man, by a good man. Someone to prove that what all the other men had already done wasn't what I deserved. My heart believed I was missing that and needed it to feel whole.

I pick up a darker shade of green and mix in an even darker shade of brown. The lake in my painting is getting murkier. It needs more darkness around the edges. I'll get to that next. It needs to reflect my reality to be therapeutic.

Before Johnny, I had been in an abusive situation with Dane. It included sexual assault and since he was an older man I still wonder if that was because of my daddy issues too, but if it was, it hadn't taught me a thing. Teenagers are thick headed when it comes to lessons. Even though Dane had lied to me in circles. Told me everything fairytales tell little girls they're looking for. Because he knew I was still fresh out of reading those, they basically gave him a roadmap into my desperately empty heart. And from there, he tore me apart. My childhood was over. Thanks Dane.

But I still needed the approving eyes of a man on me. Eyes that were attached to a body that could protect me.

The lighting in here is all wrong. I frown as I realize I haven't turned on my painting light. I walk over to the daylight lamp that's pointed at my easel with my brush still in my left hand and twist the switch with my right fingers.

"Gah," I let out the squeal and drop my brush as pain cramps the knuckles of my right had. I rub them out with my left hand but now there's paint on the carpet. I'm trying not to get mad. I'm trying to calm down. My rheumatoid arthritis is flaring up and stress is bad for that. I need an Oxy.

The doctor prescribed them to me specifically to take before strenuous activities or sex, she's told me that it's important to manage my pain in other ways too, not depend on the Oxy, but today, and more and more often recently, painting counts as strenuous activity.

I feel too young to have RA, but it turns out it can strike a person when they're in the prime of their life. It struck me at thirty-five.

I manage it well though, in general, with treatment pills, exercise, and Oxy. I do wonder if Johnny would have married me if he'd known that I'd develop this illness.

When we met Johnny was twenty-two, and to my seventeen that was exciting. Everything dangerous about him then was intoxicating. He brought all the toxic things to my doorstep, and I loved it. My blood rushed faster, I swear, for it. He placed them in my hands and my pulse pounded against his lips. I indulged on it all. Cigarettes, alcohol, guns, and the murder.

Poor animals. I still see their faces in my dreams, and it breaks my heart. I can't take back the days and the nights that I spent with Johnny then, attracted to it.

I rummage through the medicine cabinet and pull out my bottle of Oxy. Shit. It's getting low. I need a refill. I pop the pill and stare at myself in the mirror. I resent how it makes me feel, even while I love how it makes me feel better. But my adoptive mother was a pill popper. I don't talk to her anymore, but that's one of the things that sticks with me about her. Constantly throwing something back from a little yellow-and-white labeled bottle. I hate doing things that remind me of her.

My cardigan drops off my shoulder and as I slide it back up, I'm reminded that my first mother wasn't any better. My fingers play over the raised skin as the images that come with looking at the mark dance through my mind.

Red hot metal and the smell of flesh burning. Seared in my mind as pain and on my arm as a wonky stretched out heart. When you brand a child with fire and metal, the skin grows and the shape stretches, but I can still tell it's a heart. I was taken from that mother at age six and I'll probably never know why that mother did it. But she branded me and my sister, like cattle.

I had a sister that didn't come with me to my new life. I never knew what happened to her and I missed her for a long time. It's funny I don't really think about her anymore. When I do, it's a fleeting thought, in and then out. It was so long ago. So many families ago.

I cover the funny shaped heart back up with my soft sweater and sigh, the scar is a reminder that love is not always enough. It's not always the ingredient that matters. I'm sure that mother thought she loved me, but what some people label as love, is just cruel abuse and torture.

I remember the sounds when she branded my sister, that sound lives in my head, her high-pitched screams tearing into my heart and invoking this overwhelming desire to save her. But I was only a girl with no way to change anything. Maybe that's why I feel a kinship with the prey because I'm branded like cattle.

I decide to pop another Oxy. It's been a really stressful day.

I honestly can't be mad at Johnny for his murdering. He has something I don't understand because I've never had it. A heritage. Johnny thinks murder is his heritage. It's why he won't stop.

His dad did it to feed their family, and he learned it from his dad's father before that because he did the same. His dad is the one who taught him. Started taking him into the woods when he was just a kid. When his father passed away Johnny and I inherited the family cabin in the middle of nowhere, the hunting cabin.

I haven't even bothered with one of those DNA tests that will tell you everything you've ever wanted to know about your heritage. Or logged onto one of those websites. I wonder sometimes how far the website would get me. If it would help me find my sister. But then I shake my head until I forget about it. I don't want to know anymore. I don't want to know where I came from. Or what happened to the family that abandoned me. I'm over it, over all of it. If you'd have told me when I was seventeen, I'd be this over it, I'd never have believed you.

I lay down on the bed and stare at the paint stain on the carpet. I should clean it. Instead, I roll over and stare at Johnny's spot on the bed beside me. The pillow he lays his head on.

I remember our first date in detail, but not like it was yesterday, like it was a different lifetime. In a strange way, it repulses me, even though I still feel fondly when I picture it. It's such a contradiction in my mind, falling in love that way.

Johnny had asked me out when I was his waitress at the neighborhood breakfast joint. The smell of bacon grease hanging in the air. He looked so grown up sitting there, a full face of tightly trimmed stubble, eating alone, browsing a gun magazine. One hand held his coffee and the other was letting his fingers drift slowly down the glossy page.

I lingered too long after taking his order. I was staring. My tongue brushed my lower lip and then my teeth.

He noticed. He asked if I wanted him to take me hunting with him. It made my stomach flip in a different way back then. The kind of flip that comes with a racing heart and butterflies.

I said when, and he said today, why wait, life was short, and he knew the perfect place. His smile was a teasing sort. The kind that made his eyes look lazy.

I asked him if he did that kind of thing often, took girls out to the woods for a bit of light murder. He thought that was funny and when he laughed, I was hooked.

God his laugh. His two front teeth were so big and bright. His cheekbones were high, and his eyes danced with his laughter, no longer lazy but full of life.

That very afternoon, I watched him kill a rabbit for the first time, and that very evening I pressed my stomach into his side, felt the gun strapped to his belt between my legs and I fell in love. I must have kissed him a hundred times. I couldn't get enough, taking him all in. The power of it all. The control.

They say love doesn't exist at first sight. But it exists after a first date that includes guns, cigarettes, alcohol, and murder.

So long ago.

I was so young.

Oh, the naivety that exists in youth.

Things have changed drastically since then.

Samantha

**Hey Babe…Um… sorry I lost my shit.**

Johnny

**It's ok. I love you.**

Samantha

**I love you, too.**

Johnny

**I love you more.**

Samantha

**Never.**

Johnny

**I'm just saying. I do.**

Samantha

**You're always underestimating me, love.**

# Chapter Two

## LILAC

*Lilac sits in* the middle of the rectangular dining room table, her thin long golden fingers folded delicately in her lap. Her mocha brown balayage hair falls forward into her thick black eyelash extensions. She unfolds her hands to brush the shoulder length bobbed hair behind one ear and cast up her smokey-brown eyes.

The room is uncomfortably silent after her mother's outburst. Another family dinner ruined. This is exactly why they avoid family dinners regularly, and when one is planned, Lilac tries to have other plans. But her mother insisted. Like she does randomly, that they needed to sit together as a family and discuss their day and whatever it is that normal families do every night. She really wanted that. And then she went off and lost her shit and left the rest of them sitting there in uncomfortable silence.

God, it makes Lilac so angry. But as angry as she is, she doesn't throw her napkin, make a scene, and stomp up the stairs. That's crazy. Her mother is so crazy.

She scans the room, darkened by the dimmer switch attached to the chandelier above, the candle flames dance in front of her. Her mother's plate is still covered in warm food at one end, green beans, mashed potatoes, and grilled tofu. The look of it makes Lilac want to gag. Who knows what possess her mother to eat the garbage she does. Part of her mother's eccentricness. At least she doesn't force her food choices on the rest of the family.

God knows if she did, this family would never last. They'd all go their separate ways. Including Lilac. Lilac kind of feels ready to go already.

Her father sits staring down at his plate, poking his bloody meat with his fork, opposite the end of her mother's plate. A steak knife held firmly in his other hand. His wrists propped against the table while he chews. He's a quiet man, with little show of reaction to most things. It makes her feel further from him than what she really is. He's distant emotionally and she wonders what he's thinking. It hurts her feelings that he doesn't seem to wonder the same about her.

It's moments like these that she questions if she is even real. If she's just unnoticed or nonexistent.

Maybe she's a ghost in a house with two married people, convincing herself they are her parents to keep her spirit from feeling lonely. Is this what it feels like to be trapped between planes? Not realizing yet you're dead. She could imagine ghosts here in this darkened room filled with dancing shadows and candlelight. If she weren't a ghost herself, and there was one about, she'd probably feel more kinship with it than she does with her parents.

She coughs to see if her father will react. A dramatic cough, one that echoes about, as if she's choking on a piece of her meat. She doesn't want to be an actress. She's an inventor and she's happy with that. That's her career path. When people ask, what do you want to be when you grow up, she says, *oh honey, you don't have to wait until you grow up, I'm an inventor.* She's invented a piece of tech. Her dad is in tech, and her mother is detail oriented, so they helped. But it was her invention.

A pair of earrings that are Bluetooth enabled. So, ear buds are irrelevant with her earrings, and they're stylish, too.

She wears them everywhere. But since then, she's become more of a social media star rather than inventing anything else. She started doing it because she needed to market the earrings, but her social media fame is her focus now. It's morphed into just being about her and her life. Her makeup and clothes. What she does trends and that means she has influence. It takes up so much of her time. Some days she wishes she could turn it off. Leave it behind for a little bit, but then her brand would suffer. Social media doesn't allow for breaks. Breaks turn into *yesterday's news* and *irrelevant*.

But in her mind, she congratulates herself that she could be an actress if she wanted to be one. If her popularity online and her inventors path flopped.

She's sold the part of the choking girl to herself, but apparently not her father. Because he doesn't react. Takes no notice of her. He's lost in whatever is happening inside his own mind and on the phone beside him.

He only pierces his under-cooked meat and places it into his mouth. Looking over at the phone beside his plate. What if she were really choking? Would he even notice soon enough to save her life, or would he just stare at his phone while she died, writhing on the floor? She considers falling out of her chair to find out, but that would take too much commitment. She'd have to end up coughing something up then, and well, the meat is good. Plus, that may put her on the same crazy level as her mother.

"So, that was dramatic, huh?"

She defers to her mother's behavior. Surely he'll have to respond to that. He can't just ignore the sound of her voice in this vacuous room.

He looks up at her, as if it is the first time he has seen her all day.

He nods with sympathy, but not for Lilac, for her mother and her weakness.

"That's just how she is, Lilac. You know that."

She wants to keep talking, but she can see that he doesn't. He's already looked away at the bright screen on the table beside him. She tries anyways.

"She should control herself better, right?"

He doesn't answer. He touches his phone to do something there and she doesn't waste her breath repeating herself. He doesn't care.

Lilac rolls her eyes and stabs her own piece of deer with the end of her steak knife. The blood squishes out onto her plate. Bleeds into the mashed potatoes.

"That is so dumb."

Of course he defended her. She wants to say he is so dumb. Dumb for putting up with her mother's craziness. Dumb for not standing up for himself. If Lilac threw a temper tantrum the way her mother just did, he would lose his cool then. She'd be grounded for life probably.

She places the knife in her mouth and presses the sharp jagged edge against her bottom lip. It feels good. It feels like something she has control over. The metal is cool against her lip, thin between her teeth. The fear of the pain on the horizon makes her heart race. It's good to feel something.

She side glances her father to see if he's looking at her.

He isn't. Of course.

If he was looking at her, he'd see that she's tense. Her eyes are closed. Perhaps, because he's her father, he'd know something bad was about to happen. Perhaps he'd care.

Would he even care, she wonders. Would he try to stop her?

But he's not looking at her. She's alone in her conspiracy.

She pulls the knife quickly out of her mouth, across her lower lip, the jagged edge rips the soft flesh.

It hurts. It hurts more than she thought it would,

even though she'd expected, even almost craved, the pain.

She screams.

Blood spills into her plate and pours down her chin.

It's more than she imagined. It's horrifying and adrenaline pulses into her veins.

She did it. She did this and that part is exhilarating.

It tastes of salt and life, with a thick flavor that satisfies her. The pain engulfs all the other thoughts that had been roaming around in her brain a few minutes prior. The unpleasant thoughts have nothing to say now.

They're gone. It's only this. The red fountain of her own insides now mixing with her mashed potatoes, the blood pounding in her ears. The pain tearing her clean free of everything else.

"Oh my God, Lilac, are you okay?"

Her father jumps up from his chair so fast it tips over backwards and the dog, a Vizsla named Doby, barks from his place on the couch in the living room the next room over at the sudden alarming sounds. His nails on the hard wood floor mix with his concerned barks before he appears like a flash in the same room.

Everyone is alarmed. All eyes are on her. It

satisfies an animalistic craving that had been clawing at her insides.

"I'm fine, I'm fine."

She tries to catch the blood in her hands, and it drips onto her sleeve and covers her rhinestone embellished t-shirt. It's her favorite because it hugs her curves just right. But it was a small sacrifice.

Her father pulls her up into his arms and holds her. As if he doesn't even notice the blood. The blood that's now on his shirt, too. He only cares about her. She can see that now. He does care. She's reassured that he cares about her, and it warms her heart. It overflows with love back for him.

The dog barks and jumps on their legs, encouraged by the commotion. Red fur and red ears, flopping around, the red nose nudging against them, getting blood on her, too. She licks at it of course, but there are stains in places she can't reach. Behind her left ear and atop her neck on her back. Her yellow cloth collar.

Lilac's mother runs down the stairs gasping, trying to see the bloody mess. Pushing the dog down out of the crowd, she yells, "Get the keys, Jonathan! She's going to need stitches. We've got to go!"

She pushes her husband toward the key hook and wraps her arms around her daughter.

"It's okay, honey. We're here. We're going to take good care of you," she says in her soft, caring tone, and then it raises to a more demanding, louder octave, "Johnny, hurry up! Let's go!"

Through the tears that Lilac can't hold back, that are attached to the physical pain she's in, it occurs to her that she'd just been thinking her mother was weak. But now, with her arms wrapped around her this way, she's comforted because of their strength, she feels how they make her feel safe. She hears her mother's voice as it tells her father what to do and he follows her orders without question because she's the one that knows exactly what needs to be done. She is comfort and direction. She's some kind of force wrapped up in that crazy package, but Lilac understands now, that force isn't weakness.

She rests her head on her mother's shoulder and lets the tears fall onto the cream cashmere sweater that covers her, mingled with stains of her blood. The liquid drips down the sweater and falls onto her mother's jeans and Lilac relaxes.

Now her blood is on all of them.

She is alive after all.

Samantha

You think Lilac's ok? I know she's a teen
but...

Johnny

I'm sure she's fine. Maybe we should get her
back into dance?

Samantha

I was kind of thinking therapy, babe.

Johnny

No, sports are good for kids. She's been
missing something ever since she stopped dance.
I think kids need that.

Samantha

Yeah. I'm not sure she has the time. But it
couldn't hurt for her to talk to someone.

Johnny

I disagree. You know how I feel. Therapists
are looking to find something wrong. You find
what you're looking for. There's nothing wrong
with Lilac.

Samantha

**Ok.**

# Chapter Three

## SAMANTHA

*The only noise* in the sterile emergency room is a light bulb buzzing as it flickers underneath one of those bubbly flimsy plastic things in the ceiling. It's sending eerie chills of childhood school memories under the same florescent lights, down my spine.

Some emergency rooms are loud and crowded, I know because I've been to them. People packed in tightly next to each other like sardines, some crying, some bleeding, others coughing. Broken bones and hysteria. The vibes in those rooms are panic and fear. Worry that your emergency won't be emergency enough to get taken care of in time.

But ours is quiet and empty. Almost the opposite. Off-white walls and sterile smells. Absolutely no dust. As soon as you walk in the door you're being checked in and someone is rushing the patient through a big door while the family is asked to wait. It's not attached to a full functioning hospital. If someone needs an overnight stay, they must be transported to the bigger, sister hospital.

A line of cold blue faux leather chairs wrap around a wall of windows that look out to a darkened parking lot. The streetlights over the parking lot are far apart and only light up a few parking spaces each, mostly empty parking spaces, but there are few cars here and there.

Another line of chairs fills the center. But Johnny and I are the only ones sitting in any of them. I space out for a moment and start imagining one of the decorators from those house renovations shows coming in here and overhauling the whole thing. Making it a more comfortable room.

But I suppose it's this way for a reason. Easier to clean and disinfect. When someone comes in gushing blood for instance, every place that blood may touch is easily wiped down with a little bleach and then poof, it's safe for me to sit and pretend nothing bad has ever happened in the same chair I'm resting in now.

Bleach is an amazing thing. The way it makes traces of violence disappear like that. Evidence evaporates.

The thought makes me look around for blood splatter. But no. It's clean everywhere. Some janitor is doing amazing at his or her job, keeping this place free of whatever horrors may have traveled through the room of emergencies. The only proof of his or her existence is the cleanliness and the smell of bleach. Because we all know without the bleach, there would be blood here.

Johnny's hand is warm on my leg. His fingers are big, and they wrap around my thigh. The heat penetrates my black yoga pants and momentarily I'm distracted by it. It's little moments like this that make marriage worth it.

Not the sitting in the hospital waiting for our daughter to get stitches, that's not what I mean. I mean the moments where you're staring at your phone, scrolling through the thousands of comments on your daughter's social media post of her bloody lip, cut open by a knife, your stomach sick and your heart clinched, having an existential crisis about *'what kind of mother am*

*I?'* and then the warmth on your leg reminds you that you're not alone.

We're in this together. Always. Him and I.

I look at Johnny and I see he's doing the same as me. Leaning back against the chair, one hand on my thigh, the other around his cell phone. His thumb scrolling and his eyes glued to Lilac's comment section.

I touch my Bluetooth earring to make the music stop so I can talk to him.

"There are a lot of people out there that care about her, huh?"

He looks over at me and presses his lips together. It's not quite a smile, it's more of a line, but I know it's a gesture of kindness on him. An expression that says I'm here with you, for you, even when I wish I wasn't. Even when things are tough. Even when we disagree. That's why I find it attractive. That look. Though it's a feeling of disagreement behind his eyes, it's a statement of camaraderie.

"I'm not sure that's accurate."

"What do you mean?" I say, because I can see that he sees the same hundreds of comments of concern and well wishes that I see on Lilac's post. All the people and all their outpouring of love and support.

The little prayer hand emoji. The little cry face emoji. The three hearts and then the prayer hand emoji.

And then there's the ones that sound really concerned, like *'omg Lilac, that looks so bad, I can't believe that happened. Take care of yourself, the world needs you!'* and I know that reads of care, so I'm not sure what he's playing at with his 'not accurate' comment.

"Samantha."

He pauses after my name and looks at me for a long time, like he's weighing the odds of speaking his truth to me. I stare at him and wait. Another good thing about marriage. Silence isn't uncomfortable. His eyes never glance away, not like mine do, he's a straight shooter.

Mine glance to the vending machine. I never did eat. My stomach is empty and that usually makes me feisty. I'm aware of the fact that I might be hangry. I get hangry easily. My blood sugar gets *off*, though I've never officially gotten any medical recommendations on it.

"She's famous, right?" His voice is low, and he leans toward me when he says it, like he's speaking of something secretive. Even though there's nobody around to hear his apparent secret.

"Not exactly," I say, "She invented something, and she markets it by marketing herself online. I love the earrings, the social media is excessive, but is it the same as fame? Not really."

I'm not trying to understate Lilac's

accomplishments. What she did was really impressive, more than what I've ever done. But she's not famous. If she were famous, we'd have photographers following us around. They'd probably be here right now. We'd have to have extra security at our house. She'd be on TV and the tabloids. We'd be on the phone with a PR company right now trying to mitigate any bad press from this incident. Instead, she's the one exposing the incident to the public and sharing every piece of her personal life. She took the picture we're both looking at now and posted it on the internet. That's not fame. Famous people hide things like this. They protect their privacy.

"You don't consider one-point-two million followers famous?"

"What about Doby? Doby has fifty thousand followers. Do you think Doby is famous?"

"No. Doby's a dog, and I think you spend too much time on your phone."

I feel like continuing this argument with him is a waste of my time, that I need a one up to get behind me on this one, to show him an example of the fact that I'm right and he's wrong.

"Excuse me!" I call to the lady behind the emergency room desk. We can't see much of her, just the top of her hair, straight and parted down the middle, the top of her head round like the rims of her thick black glasses, which we can only see the tops of as well. I get the feeling she likes it that way. Hidden back there.

She doesn't look up; she's got a phone to her ear.

I grab Johnny's hand and stand up.

"Come on."

He rolls his eyes at me, but he follows my directions. Shrugs his shoulders. This is a good distraction for us, and he's interested in where I'm trying to go with this. He's got time to humor me. A little competition in opinions is a good distraction from the time we're being forced to wait through.

We stand in front of the lady at the front desk and stare at her blankly until she clicks the thick cream phone back down on its receiver. When she does, she looks up at me blinking her eyes faster than what's natural. Like we've been rude by waiting for her to get off the phone. Rude would have been talking over her phone call or banging my hand on the counter until she gave us her attention. But no, we waited patiently.

I already don't like her. I don't like her because of the passive annoyance she gives us for no apparent reason.

"Do you know who Lilac Rivera is?" I say curtly, and then look over at Johnny and raise my eyebrows.

"Uh... Your daughter that you just checked in

twenty minutes ago."

She looks from me to Johnny creasing the skin between her eyebrows. She shouldn't do that, there's already a line there and she's making it worse. Adding herbal tea to her diet might be helpful. Something to calm her.

"No, that's not what I mean. Do you know her outside of this encounter?"

She shakes her head and looks more at Johnny than me. She's decided she doesn't like me very much either. It's written on her face. I don't care. It's only fair because my immediate judgments of her are probably written on my face, too. Why do women do this? I'll never know. All I know is I don't like her before I ever even had a chance to feel otherwise. And she did the same thing to me.

"I don't know what you're talking about."

"Okay, Samantha, let's go sit down," Johnny says as his hand touches my elbow.

"No, I want to be clear, you don't know our daughter at all, in any way?" My voice is authoritative and direct, I acknowledge it could be nicer.

She stares at me now and sets her chin. She's openly annoyed with me, and she really has no right to be, I'm simply asking her a question. But people don't bother with whether they have a right to be annoyed or not, do they? They just get annoyed at whoever they want, all willy-nilly, all the time. Not even trying to hide the expressions on their face. If you ask me, that's what's rude.

"Why would I know your daughter?"

"My husband thinks she's famous."

"Well, I've never heard of her."

"Exactly. Thank you."

I'm ready to walk away. I'm ready to go browse the vending machine. Ease my cranky thoughts about women I don't even know. My point has been made.

Jonathan puts his finger and thumb on his eyebrows and squeezes them back and forth. He does that when he's contemplating whether whatever argument we're having is worth it. Whether he wants to keep going or not. He's weighing the worth of his win with the worth of my happiness. The win is his prey, but I'm his trophy. He's deciding where he goes from here.

"Listen. I watched a movie last week. It was a violent movie. Do you watch a lot of violent movies, Miss…" He searches her chest for a name tag but comes up short and so his search lands on her eyes with his eyebrows raised in question.

The woman behind the desk ignores his request for her name and instead answers with a simple shake of her head back and forth, like this whole ordeal is a waste of her mental space. I question my earlier judgments of her. Maybe I do like her.

"The star of the movie was Arron Gene. He's in a few action movies. Do you know him?"

The desk woman stares at Johnny for a good sixty seconds before she responds.

"Just because a man is in a movie, doesn't make him famous. Isn't famous a recognizable person? If they aren't recognizable, they aren't famous."

Oh, look at her, fighting my fight with me. Suddenly I feel camaraderie, a strength in numbers. How could I ever not like this girl? She's got gusto.

My husband laughs at this.

"So, you're trying to say you know every famous person?"

I interrupt here because I sense, like a deer in an open thicket, that Johnny has my argument in his crosshairs.

"You're young. You know social media well, am I right? Like you understand things like trending and influencer."

"That's insulting." Johnny doesn't explain why it's insulting or to whom, but I know what he means. It's insulting to him. Like he's not young enough to understand social media and that's the reason he'll lose this one. I meant it to be insulting so it seems like a good time to show him my teeth. I smile and relax my eyes at him, then turn my attention back to her.

"How many followers does a famous person usually have?" I follow up after Johnny's interruption.

"I think it depends on the age and how long they've been famous. Some famous people don't even have social media."

"Answer the question!" I raise my voice to deter the conversation from that harmful statement, bullets for Johnny's gun. I know it's worked because her cheeks flush and she stammers enough to show she's rattled. Johnny doesn't like to rattle people. He'll give a little to keep from making a scene.

"Umm, a relevant famous person today has at a minimum ten million followers on some platform. I mean really famous people have like a hundred million."

I smack the counter and look at my husband, lift my forehead with my brows, and then tilt my chin back to the helpful receptionist.

"Thank you."

I assume we're done. I've made my point, clearly. I've won and the rush makes me hot. Makes my eyelids heavy. I slide my hand around my husband's waist and rest it on his concealed weapon he has a permit to carry and pull him close to me, trying quickly to soothe his wounded ego. He hates to lose a target.

But he hasn't made eye contact with me yet and that means he hasn't conceded.

"Let me ask you something. How many followers do you have?" He's still looking at her, I'm only looking at him, I already see where he's going. The dentist tells me every time I go in that I shouldn't grind my teeth. But my dentist doesn't know what it's like being married to Johnny.

The lady behind the desk looks at her fat cream hospital phone. Hilarious that she thinks that might make it ring. I almost want it to ring for her. I feel a tiny bit bad that I brought her into this. I know Johnny and I are a lot.

"I don't know, like three-hundred and something."

"That's awesome, that's a lot, I've got one hundred and seventy-nine. My wife has four-eighty, she sells handmade jewelry. Not made by her hands of course. One of those pyramid scheme things."

Ouch, that was hurtful. He's throwing back zingers my way now. I could hand make jewelry if I wanted, too. It's just a side hustle though, I read somewhere that every woman should have a side hustle. If I'm being honest, it hasn't been working out for me like I'd expected. I think I spend more money on it than

I make from it. Not to mention the time.

"I sell makeup," she says without missing a beat. I do like her after all.

"So, what's someone with a million point two followers?"

I side glance from his eyes to hers. My breath caught in my throat. Waiting. Her answer will be the nail in one of our coffins. And 1.2 million is way more than any of the three of us have, more than what we even hope to have.

"That's just an influencer."

My lips slide across my teeth and my cheeks pull tight. I open my phone.

"What's your screen name, hun?"

She looks at me softer now. Less stern, like we've found common ground somehow.

"@Glamourshades49" she answers, trying to peak her eyes over my phone.

"Well, glamour shades forty-nine, you've got a new follower. Thank you for helping my husband and I settle this little dispute. Honey?"

I raise my eyebrows at him as I say honey and turn to go back to our seats, my eyebrows say, shall we? He looks defeated but proud of me. I love to make him proud.

He follows me back to the seats and we both go

back to our phones, this round over.

My daughter's an influencer. I had never actually labeled her that before and I let the word roll around in my brain. I've watched her internet footprint grow as the website I helped her build generated traffic. The ad campaign we did for her invention really was a success. And now, right under my nose, she's become near famous. Maybe I should be paying closer attention to what she's doing online?

Samantha

You know an influencer is basically the kid's
version of famous these days. So, you're not
wrong.

Johnny

I know.

Samantha

Do you think we should get more security at
the house?

Johnny

We have Doby.

Samantha

I mean cameras. A security company that
can alert us if something is amiss.

Johnny

Doby alerts me if something's amiss.

Samantha

Ok, Johnny. Whatever. I'm just saying.
Maybe we need some security.

Johnny
**Doby.**

Samantha
**SMH**

# Chapter Four

## LILAC

*Lilac's room is* dark with an orange glow because the lights in her emergency hospital room have been dimmed. She's supposed to be recovering from her stitches. Resting, the doctor said. Her head is foggy from the pain medication and in general she feels good. Good enough. The adrenaline rush left her satisfied, and the concern her parents showed proved they cared.

    She's slightly concerned about the scar that she may now have forever on her lower lip but the doctor promised he was very good at what he does. He told her there were two layers of dissolvable stitches and that if she kept them clean and iced them, rinsed with salt water, she'd be okay. At worst she'd have a conversation starter, he'd said.

Lilac thought that was dumb. Scars on people's faces were never conversation starters. Nobody ever walked up to someone else and said, hey, I see you have a scar there, what horrific accident lead to that permanent mark on your life and face? Maybe for a doctor it's a conversation starter, when someone comes into his ER and there's a pre-scar injury, it starts his conversation.

Dr. Scott with his red, closely shaven beard, short red curly hair and black-rimmed glasses must have little real-world experience and a lot of ER experience, which she guessed was good for her based on his age.

Lilac however is looking at the scar on her face differently. She thinks it will make her look tough. Like a tattoo, but a tattoo that a man couldn't refuse to hire her for later in life. It was kind of the perfect mark. It would say, look, I've been through stuff and I'm still standing. She'd make it say I've been through stuff and I'm still hot.

In her mind, she'd just given herself her first tattoo. It would symbolize that even when it felt like her parents didn't love her, they really did.

She's happy the doctors have finally left her room and she's resting with her head against the pillow, an IV drip attached to her outstretched left arm. They told her she didn't need to leave it outstretched, she was allowed to move it around, something about a flexible blah blah, but she was discomforted by the intrusion. She likes her space, and she certainly doesn't like something attached to her through a vein in her arm. She told them she didn't need it, but they said she did because of her blood loss. She'd rolled her eyes; it really wasn't that much blood. She'd seen worse. On TV.

Her phone is comforting and warm in her right hand as she holds it disturbingly close to her face. The bright light shining on the entirety of her face. She just finished reading all the comments on her most recent post, mostly adoring, sympathetic, and encouraging, though some were rather hateful, as always. Things like *she deserved it,* and *haha, all her pick me energy,* and the most annoying one *finally, she won't be so perfect now.*

Jealousy runs strong through the veins of humans; she's learned that the not so easy way since becoming an internet star. There's always someone desperate to make her feel bad.

Even still, she loves her followers. Most of them are kind to her, and the ones that aren't spur on comments, encouraging others to defend her, and drive her comments and views numbers through the roof. And on days when she has nothing to post for content, she can always just make a post confronting one of them. The truth is, she'd be nothing without her haters, just like she would be nothing without her fans.

That's why she'd not missed the opportunity to shock and awe her stalkers, her fans, and her haters, on the way to the hospital, blood gushing everywhere, and then she drafted a newer post, saying she was alright and showing the stitches. She refreshes her phone again to see how many more comments have appeared on the post of her split lip since the doctor left. Twenty-three new comments. She pulls the corners of her lips in an attempt to smile, but then winces. Smiling probably isn't a good idea. The doctor said not to even drink through a straw, and to only eat soft food. That seems extreme though.

She refreshes again and more comments and likes pop up on her screen, she's seeing an increase in followers. She might be going viral with this one. She'll have to wait to post the pictures of the stitches and the *I'm okay* statement. Until this post stops garnishing so much attention. A new post might steal some of this one's views or likes and that wouldn't be good for her algorithm. Not to mention all the page views coming from people clicking back in anticipation, waiting to see if she's ok.

A soft knock comes from the door before it opens, and another person dressed like a doctor comes in the room. The air-conditioning kicks on at the same time and it's like the woman brought the cold with her. Lilac didn't even say come in. She clicks the screen button on her phone to turn it off and frowns up at the woman.

It's not the same doctor who gave her the stitches. This one is a female with blonde hair that hangs in a straight line down her back and tucks neatly behind her ears. So much different from her own. Her own is a heavy dark brown, almost black, thick bob that brushes against the top of her trap muscles and shows off her collarbones. It's way too thick to ever sit behind her ears without a fuss. She's constantly brushing it back there, almost like a tick, to get it to stay. It never stays though.

"Hi, Lilac. I'm Doctor Evans."

She puts out her hand and even though it's cold, like it's been dipped in ice, it's soft and delicate in Lilac's firm embrace. Not limp, like the kind of handshake her father looks upon disapprovingly, just delicate. It has a mid-level type of authority, like she's a professional, but not a boss, and there's no aggression. Her father has taught her a lot about reading people through their handshakes. She's under the impression that he's judged every person he's ever met before they even speak to him. She knows she does.

Next is eye contact and body language. Then the tone of their voice and the level of confidence it wields.

Dr. Evans is underwhelming.

"Before we have your parents come in, I have a few questions to ask you." She tilts her chin down a half an inch and looks squarely in Lilac's solid brown eyes, "Completely private, I don't have to share this information with anyone you don't want me to. I'm only here to help you."

Lilac doesn't react. She doesn't nod her head yes, to indicate she understands. She doesn't raise her eyebrows in question. She doesn't tilt her head as if she doesn't understand. She does absolutely nothing. Sometimes sixteen-year-old girls do nothing, because they know anything can give their thoughts away. They've been trained to know that.

Lilac has been trained to know that because her father is a hunter. She is a hunter, too. He trained her to be this way. She's been doing it long before sixteen.

She's been in the woods with him as deer approach, sat perfectly still, the gun in her hands, the sight trained, the deer stepping, delicately, like this woman's handshake, closer. One step at a time. Lilac knows any movement at all can give them away.

She's listened to the crunch of dry leaves under the unsuspecting animal's hooves, the smallest twig snapping in the distance. The smell of fresh air and pine and the wind blowing their scent right up her nose, making her want to sneeze, but only one of the three things in the woods moved. The thing that ended up dead.

Any movement at all can give her away.

"First, do you feel safe at home?"

Lilac rolls her eyes then; the absurdity of the question disarms her momentarily.

"Of course, I do. What am I, ten? Are you asking if I'm afraid of the dark or being home alone? Because no. I'm not afraid of anything." Her eyes harden on the woman.

The woman creases the skin between her eyebrows and stares into Lilac's eyes with an intensity that reminds her to put her guard back up.

"Uhhh, that's not exactly what I meant. I meant do you feel safe with your parents. They aren't violent."

"Oh," Lilac laughs only slightly, not because she's humored enough to laugh, but because she wants to acknowledge the irony.

"Well, my mom calls my dad a murderer, so I'm

not sure that your statement is accurate, but he has a hunting permit so I'm pretty sure it's fine."

The woman frowns and scribbles something onto her paper and then she coughs. Her cough is delicate too, which makes Lilac wonder if it's fake.

"Plus, my mom is kind of crazy and she's taught me kickboxing personally, which isn't exactly *not violent* either, but she tries really hard to be peaceful. I give her a C for effort."

She laughs and it's an awful failure because her mouth is still numb and she can't open it very wide, it's more of just a sound repeated from her throat and pushed through her mildly parted lips with little effort.

She watches Dr. Evans try to hide the appearance of displeasure on her face.

"Have you ever tried to hurt yourself before?"

Lilac doesn't feign surprise; she goes straight to denial. She was prepared for this. She knew someone would accuse her of doing it on purpose. She just didn't know they'd have a special doctor to come in and ask.

"I didn't hurt myself on purpose. It was an accident. I cut myself with a steak knife while eating with it."

Her inflection is on the word eating, like it's the doctor's job to provide proof and eating is her alibi. She planned it that way. On the car ride to the hospital. It made sense to her quickly and she had just gone with it.

"Okay."

Doctor Evans looks down at her clipboard releasing a sigh. She's assessing. Lilac isn't the first girl to hurt herself and claim it was an accident. She knows that, she doesn't live under a rock. But if she denies it, she figures they can't prove otherwise, and then she doesn't have to go to therapy.

She knows therapy is where they send you if you try to hurt yourself because her best friend Joshua has been there and done that. He told her it was awful because some old smelly guy thought Joshua would really tell him all his problems just because he asked, and then somehow, he still left saying more than he'd meant to, and he'd even cried, right there in front of the man he didn't even know. Joshua hates crying, and so does Lilac.

The hell if she'd cry in front of a stranger.

She pictured the man Joshua had described, balding on top, with long hair growing out the sides of his head, slicked back into a low ponytail. Lilac hated him and she'd never even met him, but she hated a lot of people she'd never met. She hated radio talk show hosts that made bad jokes and then laughed at them in a room by themselves and then broadcasted the bad joke and self-applause to the world. She hated stupid politicians that acted like they were so much more important than everyone else and sat around talking shit about their colleagues all day, and then got to make decisions that affected everyone's lives; so why couldn't she hate therapists for the simple reason that one with a ponytail under a bald spot had made her best friend cry one time when he didn't want to? It seemed like a good enough reason to her.

"Lilac, you understand that most people don't cut their lip in half while eating with a steak knife, right? I don't see that a lot. In fact, I've never seen it."

"Well, you have now. I guess you think you've seen everything already."

"No, not everything."

"I'm an inventor you know. By design, I'm here to show you things you've never seen before."

The doctor pulls her red stained lips between her teeth, like she's blotting the red that's been there for hours and looks away. She's trying to hide frustration, she must be a nice person though because she lowers her voice, it somehow gets softer than it even was before. It's nearly drowned out by the sound of the industrial air conditioner.

"Honey, if there's anything you need to tell me, if you need help at home, I can help you. If you're just dealing with a lot, I can refer you to someone that can help you regularly. A lot of people need help, you'd be surprised how many. More people need help than don't, and I'd be happy to explain that to your parents with the referral as well. Okay? That's all I'm trying to do here. Give you help."

Lilac looks down before she looks back at Dr. Evans. Not with her chin, only her eyes, and only momentarily. She decides to soften her tone as well. She's ready for the conversation to be over.

"I'm fine, Doctor Evans. Really. I don't need any help."

The doctor slaps her thighs with both hands before grabbing her clipboard and standing up while letting out a convicting sigh.

"Alright. I guess I'm done here then."

She reaches out and delicately shakes Lilac's hand goodbye. Lilac's father might not have disapproved of the handshake, but Lilac does. A woman shouldn't shake a person's hand like she's prey. As delicately as a deer walks. She rolls her eyes behind the woman's back as she walks away and picks her phone up out of her lap.

The cold air coughs and splutters and rattles as it finally turns off, just as Dr. Evans leaves.

"That poor woman," Lilac mutters. "The cold just follows her around like that."

There's a private message from Tom.

*Oh, thank God* she thinks. Her heart races, relief floods her veins.

She didn't just get her parents attention, she didn't just get the internet's attention, she'd gotten Tom's attention as well. This night just keeps getting better. Maybe the local news will even do a story on her. She should send them a press packet with photos and statements.

**You ok, love?**

**Yes. Yes. It was nothing. Just an accident.**

**I missed you, babe.**

It's been three weeks since Tom ghosted Lilac. She missed him, too. But there's no bloody way she's telling him that. Absolutely no way. He thinks he can string her along for three weeks without saying a thing to her and then when he shows back up she'll be all desperate for him. Well. He's right. But she knows better than to show him her desperation. Desperation is a form of weakness. It was her mother that taught her that.

When Lilac messages back she pretends she

didn't notice it's been three weeks.

**Missed me? Did you go somewhere?**

He takes a while to respond to that. He doesn't know what to say, she's sure of it. And that makes her warm, she wants to smile but she won't. Self-control. Her tongue feels the fresh stitches in the back of her lip. Her mouth tastes sterile and she wants some ice chips but nobody's around.

**No, I just haven't talked to you in a while. Figured you were busy.**

**Yeah, I have been. I didn't even notice.**

**Oh. Ok.**
**Your lip okay. I saw your in the hospital.**

**It's \*you're in the hospital. And I'm fine. But that's insider information. Don't tell.**

**Oh, I get insider information?**

**Only because you're my favorite.**

She stands up and stretches, she feels so good she wants to jump in the air and clap her hands, but she'll settle for hitting the call button. She wants to go home. She's done it. She's gotten Tom back. She really had missed him. She'd thought of him every day. And every night, too. She'd stalk his page when she'd turn out the lights and lie in her bed, nothing but a t-shirt on under her sheets. She even bought a t-shirt that looked just like one of the ones he had in one of his pictures. She found it at the skater shop where she knew he shopped. When she wore it she pretended it was his.

He kept posting every single day, four or five times, just like a good influencer, so she knew he'd been ghosting her. It made her heart ache at night. Once she got tired of scrolling his pictures and reading all the girls' comments, she'd plug in her phone and pray to God that he'd come back to her.

She'd cry and scream silently into her pillow. The kind of scream that nobody can hear but she knew a God somewhere could feel. Because it hurt so bad.

**I'm only allowed to eat soft foods for a while. So, I guess I'm vegetarian like my mom now.**

**You could always drink a meat smoothie Yum.**

**Gag. That sounds disgusting. I think I'll pass.**

**Tofu sounds disgusting to me.**

**Yeah. I won't be eating that. I'm thinking skinny ice cream.**

**That's what I'm talking about.**

The several times Lilac had messaged Tom in the middle of the night, after she'd cried so hard she couldn't find sleep to save her soul, sitting on read without reply, right above their current conversation, makes her flush. But she ignores the words.

The *Hi!*

The *Hey, where you at?*

The *what you doing, hottie?*

She just goes on pretending that she didn't even notice he'd never responded. It doesn't matter now anyway, whatever his distraction had been, was gone now. At least at this moment.

Maybe a real-life girlfriend. Someone in his town. Or someone that would be close enough to see him sometimes. Maybe Tom needed more than words and pictures.

She starts feeling sad and guilty that she can't give him more.

The more her mind spirals down that rabbit hole the more she starts panicking she'll lose him again. She's so far away.

And her parents will never take her to go see a man three states away.

They will never let her drive by herself.

Shit.

She is going to lose him again. As soon as the popularity of this incident calms down, he'll ghost her again for someone he can actually touch. Someone he can let his eyes travel over with his hands following suit.

She is suddenly overwhelmed with certainty that Tom's lips have been on someone else's pouty pink stained lips, and it makes her stomach turn, it makes her heart sink.

There is nothing she can even do.


**I actually did miss you a little, too.**
**Just a little.**
**While I was really busy.**

**I knew it!**
**I think it's hot when you show that your a**

**human with an actual heart.**

**\*You're**

**LOL. OMG. SMH.**

Lilac smiles.
And then she immediately regrets it.

Samantha

When do you think they'll let us see Lilac?

Johnny

Any minute, babe. Don't worry.

Samantha

It's been kind of a long time.

Johnny

You're a good Mom. I love you.

Samantha

I'm so glad you can spell you're right.
Can you imagine us making it if you
couldn't?
Lol.

Johnny

Same honestly.

# Chapter Five

## SAMANTHA

*I'm not sure* what I expected to see when the hospital led us back into Lilac's room.

A small little girl with braids on each side of her head and bows at the end of each braid. Tears in her eyes. A baby running into my arms from a sterile hospital bed that was too big for her. Screaming my name like I was her hero, and it was a crime they kept her from me.

I meant to sweep her into me and breathe in the

smell of her head, which I don't spend enough time breathing in anymore.

I don't know when it happened. One day I am spending hours with her little head snuggled against me, that sweet scent triggering my maternal instincts and the next day I'm just standing here, staring at her awkwardly, knowing it would be awkward if I even tried.

She hasn't been that girl for a long while.

And yet, I was still hurt when she didn't look up from her phone. Didn't care whether I was even there. Typing with her thumbs, staring at the screen. She hadn't been missing me at all. Hadn't noticed they'd been keeping me from her. No tears or heartbreak without me. I guess that's typical teenage behavior, but I don't like it. My brain doesn't accept it.

So, I'd rushed over to her bedside and threw my arms around her. After standing there. Awkwardly waiting for her to look up and acknowledge me. A slightly alarming beeping coming from a room down the hall. The smell of lemon scented bleach permeating every molecule of oxygen in the air.

"Lilac!"

I'd pulled myself back to look in her eyes and brushed the hair behind her ears the way she always does. Like she wasn't capable of doing it herself.

Pretending as if nurturing her in that way was more for her than me.

"Are you ok?" I'd said with all the compassion inside me.

She'd squirmed away from me, if I didn't know better, I'd say she seemed repulsed.

"God, Mom. I'm fine. It's just stitches."

So, I don't think it's strange that I'm pretending to get an eyelash out of my eye just to watch her through the visor mirror, in the backseat of our car, still pounding away with her thumbs on her phone. Why is that stupid little square, tiny computer, more important than me? Her own mother?

Maybe it was a mistake buying that thing for her when she was ten. She'd begged for it so aggressively. Johnny and I had always had a hard time telling her no, and when she'd activated the puppy eyes and told us a sap story of how her best friend had one and she needed it to keep in touch because her friend had just moved to California, I'd told her she could just use mine to call her friend, Emmy, but the next holiday, Lilac's birthday, I'd bought her the phone. And now look. It's more important than me. I should have known.

"Honey, who are you talking to on your phone?"

"Nobody, Mom. You know I have to reply to my comments on my page to stay engaged. The algorithm likes that. It makes me feel personable."

The thing is though, like I said before, I've been watching her comment section, and she hasn't replied to any of them. She's lying to me.

I open my own phone with a click and a smile, to make sure that nothing has changed. Her photo was the last thing I looked at, so it just takes a quick refresh to see, that no, she still hasn't replied to anything. She's keeping her followers in suspense and they're taking the bait, hanging on to the possibilities.

My loud sigh causes Johnny to look over at me. I shake my head at him, telling him she's lying through my movement, then snap the visor closed and look out my passenger window.

I'm losing it with Lilac, the special Mother-Daughter bond we used to have. She couldn't care less what I think, what I say, or how she treats me. She doesn't care that inside this little vehicle flying down the road at twenty-nine miles per hour with the world passing by outside I'm the one that loves her, and Johnny of course, but not all the people inside that dumb rectangle screen. And she'll lie to me. Without even a second thought. Because they're more important now.

Ever since she became influential.

Ever since she invented a pair of earrings.

I turn up the radio dial. Let the music voice my anger and frustration. Let it drown out the voice in my head telling me how far the gap between mother and daughter is. How it's turned into a canyon during some natural disaster I must have slept through.

I'm the one who pulled all the strings for her. Hooked her up with a lawyer, got her patents and production. She thinks she's smarter than me now. Not completely a-typical for a sixteen-year-old, but her invention would be little more than an idea without me.

Still, that's what mothers are for, I guess. Be the wind beneath their children's wings. Even after they've forgotten their wings need wind, too.

I just wish she'd spend any time at all being appreciative.

Or at least act like she still cares about me.

That's not really asking too much is it?

"I love you, Lilac," I say over my shoulder into the backseat.

She doesn't answer. Maybe it's my fault. Maybe it's the music.

"I love you, Lilac!" I say this time louder, more aggressively.

"Huh?"

She finally looks up from her phone to make eye contact with me.

I roll my eyes and look away.

I guess this is motherhood. It's not like I wasn't warned about having teenagers. That it would be tough. It's not like I wasn't a tough teenager myself. Maybe this is what I get. What I deserve. Maybe I deserve this because when I was Lilac's age, after I left the job my mother had forced me into with Dane, I left her. I got the waitressing job and I convinced Dane to sign a rental agreement for me at a roach infested apartment complex. I told him I'd go to the police about what he'd done to me, a minor, if he didn't. And I'd washed my hands clean of both of them then. The mother that had adopted me. And Dane. I pretended like neither of them existed. Like all that damage wasn't buried inside of me. And so, I guess, now, it shouldn't surprise me to see Lilac in the backseat pretending like I'm not here. Karma. Maybe it's what girls that age do. At least she still lives under my roof. At least I haven't damaged her.

Samantha

What do you think Lilac is doing on her
phone?

Johnny

Girl stuff.

Samantha

She didn't even care whether we were there
or not. Did you notice that?

Johnny

Yes she did. She's just a teenager.

Samantha

Ok.

# Chapter Six

## LILAC

*In her bedroom,* Lilac moves slowly through the kickboxing movements her mother has taught her. The physical strength of most women is in their legs. That's what her mother says. If you need to defend yourself in the street and don't have a weapon handy, use your legs. Her mother is always thinking about things like that. Lilac doesn't know why though. She just knows her mother believes it's important for girls to know self-defense. She suspects it has something to do with that crazy heart scar on her mother's arm. Her mom won't talk about how she got it, but it makes a statement. Like she told the doctor lady, her mother gets a C for effort when it comes to being peaceful.

But, if she's being really honest, she does find kickboxing peace inducing. Like some people use Tai Chi. When Lilac is focused on her movements and refinement of her muscles, she finds her center in her strength.

Her phone pings from her bed as she roundhouse kicks the air.

Lilac's a good girl and she never meant to start sexting. She doesn't even like the name sexting, it seems inappropriate. But she knows that's what her and Tom do together. That's what her friends would call it. But several of her friends have actually had sex, and that's so far from what her and Tom have done. The word shouldn't even be in the title of what they do. They've never even seen each other in person.

It's just pictures and words typed in a room that's empty.

She's never felt his breath on her face or ran her hand down his arm. She's never stared directly into his eyes and whispered that she loved him. Though she's imagined it a hundred times. In a hundred different scenarios.

The room is getting stuffy from body heat now. Even though her workout is slow, because of her stitches she's only moving through the movements in exaggerated slowness, working on balance and refinement of technique, she's still raising her body temperature.

She crosses the room and opens a window before grabbing her phone to see what Tom's sent.

Lilac hasn't had sex with anyone before, so it feels like she's overstating the loss of her innocence to say the two of them are sexting. But she wants to keep Tom. She does and says everything she can to make sure he comes back to her when he gets home in his bed, she wants him thinking about her. Not someone closer. Not someone he can smell. Can taste. Can touch. She wants it to be her. All her.

So, she takes things further in the messages and stretches her imagination, but at the end of the day it's all pretend. Imagination and make believe. But the pictures are real. She'd never send fake pictures and she knows Tom wouldn't either.

She can trust him. He's not a creep or a too cool to be real type of guy. She's got good senses and knows how to trust them. That's her hunter heritage.

She lays down on her bed and crosses her ankles before responding.

Sometimes she wonders if what she's doing is bad. And if it is, how bad. The Bible says nothing about sexting. Sexting isn't sex. It's a made-up name for something that didn't even exist in the time of Jesus, or even in her parents' childhood for that matter.

Would the church disapprove? Probably. She could ask at confession if she still went to confession. But she doesn't.

And she definitely isn't going to ask her mom or dad.

God, just imagining what her father would do to Tom, if he knew about the pictures they have sent each other, makes her stomach turn.

**Lilac? Are you there?**

**Hey babe.**

**I'm horny. Are you?**

Tom didn't use to start off his conversations like a pervert. If he had, Lilac would have blocked him immediately, even with his attractive profile. Because perverts are not her thing. She has to block them constantly. Being an influencer, it comes with the territory. Them and their dick pics and their sleazy comments. What she and Tom have is different.

Lilac and Tom have had all the romantic conversations already. They've talked about their favorite sports and favorite movies.

She knows he wants to be a professional skateboarder and she believes in him and his dreams. He's told her his fears of failure and she's encouraged him to push through his fears. Inspired him with her stories of success and how she pushed through her fear.

They've had dinner together, at the same time. And watched the same movie at the same time.

He makes her laugh and he's made her cry, but the laughing part is the best part, and she wants to keep him.

They just haven't met in real life because Tom lives in Utah and Lilac lives in Washington.

**I'm horny. And I'm alone.**

**God, you're so hot.**

**I'm bad, too. Do you like that?**

**You know I do.**

She fluffs the pillows up behind her and swipes

to Tom's profile and browses his pictures. He's eighteen, which makes him two years older than her, and bigger than most of the boys in her grade. His muscles are more developed, and he has stubble on his face when he doesn't shave for a few days. The pictures with stubble make her heart race. Especially when his hair is down and curls dangle into his eyes.

He loves the skate park and has three main friends he hangs with, making skater videos and posting them to his page. He's the hottest of the four.

**What are you wearing?**

**Maybe you should ask what I'm not wearing.**

She likes to tease him a bit. That's what led to the sexting. Honestly, Lilac doesn't even know if it's called sexting if it's over private message instead of text.

But it started with her, not him. She sent him the first picture. It was a picture of her top half. No shirt. Lots of lipstick. And a lace bra.

She'd been staring at his chiseled abs in the hot sun with his sharp jawline and shaggy brown hair. He'd posted the picture that day. She had decided that she needed to make him feel the way that he was making her feel inside. She'd thought it wasn't fair that she should feel like this, and he could go weeks without even talking to her. So, she'd sent him the first topless photo. She wasn't completely topless; she'd been wearing a bra.

That time.

**Okay. What aren't you wearing?**

**Be more specific.**

**Are you wearing pants?**

No.

**Shorts?**

No.

**Underwear?**

Yes.

**A t-shirt?**

No.

**A tank top?**

No.

**Are you wearing a shirt?**

No.

**A bra?**

No.

**Oh my God, I'm dying over here.**
**Send me a fucking pic.**
**You're killing me.**

Of course, she's lying about what she's wearing. But she has some pictures saved just for him. She's taken lots over the three weeks he ghosted her. She was hoping she'd get the chance to send them. She was terrified she wouldn't. There were nights she had done a whole photo shoot locked in her bedroom, just for him, as a distraction from the reality that he wasn't talking to her. Then when she'd finally finished editing, saved them to a folder with his name on it, and the lights were off, that's when she would cry the hardest. She had been lost without him.

Lilac sends him lots of pictures now. And he sends some, too. Just for her.

Pictures that would make her father hunt Tom down.

And God knows what her father would do to him.

# Chapter Seven

## SAMANTHA

Day 1

*Johnny and I* used to make love before he went off on a weeklong hunting trip. Hot and passionate love that made us feel like we were the only two souls in the world that belonged together. Like our bodies were desperate to melt into each other.

I'd hold him like he might never come back. He'd kiss me before dawn and I'd raise my eyelashes extra slow, batting them at him with sleepy eyes. His lips trailing down my neck and across my collarbone.

I relished in it back then, they were my favorite mornings. The mornings I'd drift off in daydreams thinking about when he was gone, and I missed him. When I thought about them, I could still feel the heat in my skin, and I'd get that warm feeling in my chest that made a lazy smile come to my face.

Now he disappears with the sunrise, and I never see either, the daydreams or the sunrise. I do miss the sunrise, the same way I miss those passionate mornings. I could surely have both, if I'd just open my eyes when I hear him rustling out of our sheets. It's different now though. Now that I have RA. Mornings are hard for me. My whole body is stiff with pain, and I wake up slowly. I move slowly until I get my pain meds. Everything is hard in the morning.

So truthfully, I like it this way. I'm too tired. Too tired to care about colors in the sky, and too tired to make love to a man on his way out the door to murder. I'd rather just lie in bed. With my eyes closed. As if neither exist. As if I don't know any of the details. Ignorance is bliss but pretending ignorance is second place.

Better than talking about it. Better than fighting. Better than pretending I'm ok with all of it. That's part of marriage, too. I think every couple has their closets that they keep their skeletons in, subjects that they just tuck away and don't talk about with each other. And I'm sure we aren't the only ones with his and hers closets.

This is our love language now, and this is the way a marriage evolves. I drive him crazy until he leaves in the early morning. Quietly dressing and preparing his guns, being careful not to wake me. Knowing if he does, I'll be extra grumpy because I'll be in pain and I won't have had my Oxy crutch yet, he might get a lecture about growing out of hunting the way I've grown out of eating meat. But he would know the lecture is just my way of begging him to stay, and neither of us want that.

I want him to go. I want him to do the things that make him happy, and I don't want to be the reason he doesn't do the things that make him happy. So, I sleep through the sunrise.

And after he's gone, I do enjoy my time alone. Appreciate the ability to sleep in and not hear his snores waking me. Not see his face judging me if I sleep too late. I like it when our house is quiet. The same way he likes the quiet in his stand in the trees. It's too bad we can't enjoy the quiet together. But never mind that. It's different when there's quiet between two people when they're together.

It must be the alone type of quiet for either of us to enjoy it.

I roll over to look at the clock and see that it's almost noon. The dog probably needs to go out, and Lilac's breakfast dishes are probably on the table, waiting for me to carry them off to the sink and wash them. I wonder for a minute if maybe she stayed home from school today. Given the excitement of the weekend.

I hold my breath and listen for sounds. Water running or dishes clinking. Loud music coming from a room that's locked from the inside. But there is nothing. Just the quiet. I inhale a deep, grateful breath and roll onto my back. The dog knows that's her sign and she jumps to my face and covers it with desperate kisses. Hoping if she wets it thoroughly enough, I'll rise and let her out in the yard.

I push her to the floor and groan because she's right. I will. I shuffle around, finding my robe and fluffy slippers, pop the pill that's on my nightstand, and walk her to the back door. Finally, she is outside, and now I'm truly alone. The moment is magical. God, I love to be alone. I feel guilt for that, and I don't know why. Maybe because the people I love expect me to prefer their company, but I can't help how I feel. I love the energy of the room when it's only my energy. And maybe that's because I'm the one everyone else is always asking to do something for them.

The thought makes me glance at the kitchen table. Expecting to see Lilac's breakfast dishes there.

It's empty. The entire table is empty and clean.

A stranger might not see this as meaning anything at all. May not understand why it throws me off balance. But in my house, the table is never clean in the morning. The dishes sit there, and they wait for me. They wait for me to rise and sweep them away to the sink. I'm the one that cleans my family's messes. This is my job.

I walk to the sink.

There is nothing in the sink either.

"Hmm." I break the silence of the room with this simple noise. It shouldn't be a big deal, I think to myself.

But something feels wrong. It feels off.

It's completely possible that Lilac skipped breakfast. Even though she never skips meals. In fact, she has so many meals, it's more fair to say that she never stops eating. She's a snacker.

But maybe it's her lip, I realize. Maybe it was too hard for her to decide what to eat since she must stick to a soft diet. Maybe she got something on the way to school in a drive thru. Something she can drink. Or maybe she skipped breakfast all together.

I nod my head, deciding that must be it and smile

because that's one less thing I have to do today.

Doby lands her paws on the back door and barks, distracting me from my unease. I make a mental note that I need to go to the store and stock up on foods Lilac can eat or drink easily during her recovery.

I open the back door and let Doby come crashing in. Her golden-red hair sweeping through the door like the model she is. I grab my phone and snap a photo for her Instagram. I feed her. And I head upstairs to peek into Lilac's room. Just to make sure she isn't still sleeping.

I open the door, and it is empty.

The bed is made, and the floor is clean.

"What in the... actual... hell?"

I'm so confused now I look behind me. Like maybe I'm being pranked. Maybe this is a joke. But there's nobody there.

Can a person get a concussion from cutting their lip? Can personalities change overnight? I back out of the room and stare at it from the hallway. Maybe Lilac is feeling like she needs to make some life changes? Maybe she's having a Motivation Monday. Maybe this was all for a social media post?

I shake my head. Deciding I don't care. Because I actually like that Lilac has cleaned up after herself. If this is what age kids start cleaning up after themselves, sixteen, then I've been misled by other mothers of teenagers. But most likely this is a one-time thing, and I'm just going to enjoy the moment.

When I climb out of my bubble bath, I realize that the sun has started giving way to the end of the day and the room is darker than it was a few minutes ago. The color of dusk. A grayish type of blue. It's been a beautiful day of nothing but me time and I'm lavishing in the silence but I'm starting to wonder where Lilac is. We have a rule about being home before dark. And though she seems to believe rules don't apply to her, I know that it's getting close to curfew, so getting out my mom voice may be something I have to do soon.

My sweats are in the bottom drawer of our dresser and I'm so relaxed in them that I fall into my unmade bed. The comforter still rumpled and the sheets in a ball at the bottom of the bed. Who even uses sheets anymore? Johnny does, that's who. Following in his father's footsteps with every step he takes, never mind the times and what everyone else is doing. He's a young man, but he's old fashioned.

I never make the bed when Johnny's gone. It's one of those things that make me feel rebellious. That makes his vacation a vacation for me. So, I leave the sheets at the bottom of the bed and pull the rumpled comforter around me. Fluff the pillows under my head and push Johnny's back onto his side of the bed.

I pull my phone off the nightstand and begin to browse through my social media apps. I land on Lilac's page because all the apps know she's my favorite and I'm her number one fan and am shocked to see that she's posted nothing today. Maybe she really has decided to make some changes.

Five times a day is her minimum. She's told me so many times about the algorithm and the need for specific numbers and I've told her back that taking a break is okay sometimes. These poor kids and the pressure these apps are putting on them.

She must be finally listening to all the things I've been saying to her. That she'd feel better if she spent some time away from her screen. That cleaning up after yourself makes you feel better about yourself as a person. I'm so proud of myself and my ability to be a good mother and raise such a bright young woman, an inventor, an influencer, and now a young lady that is setting boundaries for herself and leaving an organized polished presence in her wake, that I decide I won't call her and yell at her for being late.

And the last thing I think before the light on the screen of my phone, and the motion of the swiping, lulls me to sleep is that I'm such a good mom, and damn, it's been a really good day.

I wake at two am and all the lights in the house are still on. That's annoying. If Lilac was going to come home late, she could at least turn off lights. Then I laugh at myself, because yeah, she can't be perfect. I stumble out of bed, and the dog jumps up, too. She wags and kisses, and I realize that I've also not let her out before bed. So, I head for the lights, and the bathroom, and the back door. I rub my hand over the scar on my arm because it itches sometimes at night.

I pop some much-needed pills.

When I head back upstairs to get into my bed and I see the light streaming out from under the crack in Lilac's door, I knock lightly. There is no response, and I didn't expect there to be. It's normal for her to fall asleep with the light on. Her bluetooth earrings in and her laptop on her bed.

I push the door open gently, and when her bed comes into view my heart drops into my stomach. It's still empty. The bed is still made. Purple lilacs embroidered across the top of her white comforter with no wrinkles, as if it's been pressed. She's never been in it. It's two am and she hasn't even rested on top of it. There's a glass of water that hasn't been touched in the same place under the warm light of the lamp like it was this morning.

I feel sick. Something's wrong, nothing about this is right.

"Lilac?" I call quietly at first, and then as the sound echoes back to me, I yell, "Lilac? Are you here?"

I already know the answer because I've already been through the house, but it doesn't keep me from racing to each room, calling her name and flipping back on all the lights.

Memories of the entire day start dropping into my mind like spilled Legos on the floor I can't help stepping on. The absent breakfast dishes, the clean room, the social media hiatus, and the curfew call that never came.

Shit.

How long have things been wrong and I didn't even notice.

All day? Since last night?

"Lilac!" I yell one more time. Panic threatening to overtake me. I can't think. I can't process. I'm not sure what to do.

I run back to my nightstand and I grab my phone, I call Lilac first but it goes straight to voicemail.

"No. No. Answer your phone."

I call two more times with no change. The phone rings once and then I hear her voice, "I'm sorry I can't take your call, don't leave a voicemail, I'll never hear it, send a text, you weirdo."

On the third try I leave a voicemail anyways, "Lilac! Answer your damn phone!"

I'm going to throw up. I'm actually going to vomit right here. I have no idea what to do. I'm alone in this house. For the first time, I feel too alone.

I send the same message I left as a voicemail in text form so she can see it. The bubble is blue after I send it and that means what I knew it meant the first time her phone went to voicemail; her phone is either turned off or dead.

I try to call Johnny. The same thing happens with his phone, and I knew it would. He never gets cell service when he's out hunting. He'll be gone all week and he won't get a single call or text from me. I yell at his overly polite voicemail message, "Johnny! It's fucking two am and your daughter isn't home, and her phone is dead, and if you weren't so obsessed with murder maybe you'd know that, but you don't because for fuck's sake." I hang up before saying anything completely coherent because my heart feels like it's going to beat out of my chest.

I'm blaming Johnny but I'm mad at myself. I should have noticed something was wrong sooner. First thing this morning. Maybe if I had gotten up to see the sunrise and fucked my husband nothing would even be wrong. Maybe I could have prevented whatever this is altogether.

I try to breathe. Tell myself I'm overreacting. I'm pacing the hallway and then I divert into the bathroom and vomit.

Should I call the police? I've never had to call the police before. I'm not really a "call the police" kind of person. I've kind of been conditioned by social media and the news to believe they aren't really on my side. I'm kind of scared of them showing up at my house in the middle of the night. But who do I call? I need to talk to somebody. I need to tell somebody that my daughter isn't home, and she should be.

"Fuck."

I throw my phone down on the bed and storm angrily into the closet to get my shoes.

Driving around in the pitch black of morning, tears start leaking from my eyes. As soon as they do, more come, faster and harder, wrinkling my nose and forcing me to gasp for air. I'm losing it. The anxiety has transformed itself into a sad kind of fear over the past two hours and I've driven down every street in our suburb and knocked on every one of Lilac's friend's doors. Nobody has seen her or heard from her. Her car hasn't been in any driveway, or any parking lot and I've run out of places to check.

I pull into my driveway and turn off the car. I stare at the house that's as bright as a runway with every light turned on. I pull my phone out of my purse, knowing there's nothing left to do but to call the police. But before I do, I decide to check the house one more time. Maybe she's inside this time. Even though I already know. Because her car is not in the driveway with mine.

I open the door and call Lilac's name. There is nothing but silence and Doby jumping on me. I sink to my knees and cry into her silky red fur. She pees. I don't even care. For a moment I feel the urge to yell at Doby, to tell her she's the worst dog, but I know it's my fault, I didn't follow the *ignore and walk to the back door* protocol.

So, I just get to my feet, ignore the pain in my joints, step over the pee, and sink onto the couch.

My fingers do the calling the police for me. I can't even process the action. The operator's voice is a fuzzy weak thing coming from my phone.

"911. What is your emergency?"

"My daughter's missing."

"How old is she?"

"She's sixteen."

91

"How long has she been missing?"

"I'm not sure, she didn't come home at her curfew."

"And what time is that?"

"Dark."

"So, she's been missing since dark?" The call operator's voice digs through the anxiety blaring in my brain.

"I don't know."

"What do you mean? Ma'am? Did you see her before dark?"

"She didn't come home from school. But she doesn't always come home from school."

"Of course, ma'am, she's a teenager, this is very common. Teenagers do these kinds of things. So, you saw her before school?"

"No. No I didn't."

"So, she's been missing since before school?"

"No. I. I don't know. She cleaned her room and didn't leave a breakfast mess."

"Oh. Okay. That sounds like we may be looking at a runaway. I'm going to send an officer out to your house. Do you want to stay on the line with me until they get there?"

"No." I answer flatly. In my head I'm arguing with her. I'm telling her Lilac would never run away. But what do I know? I don't even know how long she's been missing.

I'm a terrible mother.

# Chapter Eight

## LILAC

Day 1

*Lilac pulls into* a gas station she's never been to; in a place she doesn't recognize. She's got all the cash she stole from her mother's purse and all the cash she had folded in half, stashed here and there, in jean pockets and dresser drawers. She doesn't want to use her debit card because she's seen enough television to know those are easily tracked. She's not ready to be tracked.

Her legs are tan and long and her skirt skimpy.

She has to look her best. She'd spent hours getting ready in the darkness before dawn this morning. She's wearing a sweater on top and a jean jacket over the sweater. When she opens her door at the pump and slides her legs from the driver side door she catches the man at the pump across from her gawking. His eyes start at her ankles and travel up her smooth tan skin until they stop and linger on her skirt as it moves, probably not covering what it should as she pulls herself up out of her seat.

She waits for his eyes to make it up to her stony expression. Stands there in her wedged sandals with both hands on her uneven hips. When they finally get there he smiles, apparently happy that he's caught her attention to.

"Fuck off!" she yells across the space between them. Loud enough everyone around them can hear. She doesn't feel like having a private conversation. She wishes she could block perverts in real life as easily as she can on her phone.

She walks around the car to the station attendant and pays cash, when she gets back to her gas tank she makes eye contact with an older woman who is smiling slyly at her. She must have heard Lilac make a scene. The woman nods and winks and Lilac knows instantly that's what her mother would have done. It's then that she starts to feel guilty. Just a hint. It's the first time she's given her actions a second thought. She wouldn't let herself even glance in that direction inside her mind before now, because if she did, she knew she might not follow through. And she wants to follow through. She wants to do this so desperately that she took every ounce of fear she had about it and stuffed it deep in her chest under anger, resentment, and feelings of how unfair life was being to her by keeping Tom so far away.

The guilt she feels now is still so small next to the excitement. The excitement of being out in the world. The excitement of pushing so far past her boundaries that she feels free of them. Beyond their reach. Untouchable. A feeling of freedom she's never felt before. Not with cell phones, and tracking apps, and social media. She feels like someone is always watching all the time, but now, now she feels free. Hidden from all the eyes that are always on her.

She's just some girl, any other girl nobody knows, standing at a gas pump filling her tank and everyone around her has no idea who she is. But they're still looking at her. She smiles and winks back at the middle-aged lady as she places the nozzle inside her tank to fill up.

This feeling of finally taking control is intoxicating and she wants more of it. She's not even close to finished with it. If she could turn this feeling into a drink and chug it, she would. She may even become an addict. Start popping it the way her mom does pain pills.

Joshua, Lilac's best friend, says she's attention seeking. Maybe he's right. It's something that she asks herself often. She knows that she craves it. That it's something she feels like she needs. But to be successful in this world these days, it is something you need. She's only sixteen and she can see that plain as day, and that just means she's smart. It's just another reason she's making it in this world while others aren't. Joshua just doesn't see how important and imperative attention is yet.

And would it be too much to ask for her parents to pay more attention to her, too? She's an inventor. How many girls her age have a career already? Not just a career, but a successful one. Yes, a lot of her friends are getting jobs. But she's got one that has earned her a savings account full of college money and an online following of over a million people. That should be enough. But it's not. It's not enough to make her parents ask her how her day is or to take any interest in her love life. It's not enough for Tom to call her every morning and every night. She wants more. She doesn't know how much more attention she needs. But she does know it's more than what she gets. Because she doesn't feel whole yet. She doesn't feel loved. And she craves the feeling of love.

She craves it so deeply some nights she feels like it's going to swallow her up. When she's lying there in bed, and nobody has checked on her. When Tom hasn't called her or messaged her in weeks. When she scrolls through the comments on her post and realizes none of those people really know her. The craving for love feels like it will kill her.

Sometimes she feels like Tom loves her. When he says he can't get enough of her. When he begs her for more time or more pictures. But then he disappears. Ghosts her. Like he just did this past month, and she realizes she didn't give enough. Didn't do enough to keep his attention on her. To garnish his undying, unrelenting love for her. The kind of love she wants to give him. Will give him.

When he sees her in this outfit. In person. And he gets to touch her. He'll never leave her again.

She sees love like a plant. And Tom is a seed, and she is the sun and the water, and if she can figure out, just the right amount of both to give him, his love will grow into something magical, and it will be just what she's always wanted. His fruit is exactly what she needs to quench this unyielding thirst.

And that's why she had to go. Go on this road trip.

When he asked her last night.

After she'd sent him the pictures. He said, "Come." Not cum. But come.

**Come to me. Here. I need to see you. In real life. I need to touch your face. To put my hands in your hair. I want to hold you in my two arms and press my lips softly against your cheek.**

**If I do, will you teach me to skateboard?**

**Of course. I will teach you anything you want.**

**Promise?**

**Lilac. If you come here, I'll give you everything I could possibly give you in one lifetime. Because you are all I want. So come to me.**

**I'm on my way.**

He had never sounded so romantic. So desperate. So much in love. He was usually so cool. Danced around romantic words to sound laid back and cocky. She knew it was a sproutling and she needed to water that sproutling right then and there if she wanted it to grow. So, she grabbed her purse, her spare cash, swiped the cash in her mom's purse, grabbed her car keys and left.

She knew her mom would be mad, but she hoped that after she'd done this, after some time and some space, after she had time to cool down, she'd understand. That's why she made her bed and cleaned her room, to say she was sorry, and she hoped that if she got back before her father's hunting trip was over, he'd never even have to know. Because her father would be less understanding undoubtedly. Her father scared her when his temper flared. Which was rarely. But she was his little girl. The spitting image. She was only scared of his temper because Mom always brought up how capable he was of killing.

The gas pump clinks off indicating her tank is full. The lady on the other side's tank clinks off at the same time. They make eye contact and smile before continuing on with the basic task of completing the transaction.

Once back in the driver's seat she turns on her phone for a moment to check her maps.

Tom's house showed exactly thirteen hours away

from hers before she left. From her suburb to his. Thirteen hours isn't that far. Less than one whole day. And maybe this trip is everything she needs. Imagining the excitement of seeing Tom's face when she pulls into his driveway bubbles beneath the anxiety. It overtakes her fear and the guilt she feels for not telling her parents.

She isn't just a dreamer. She's a dream maker. She doesn't just wait for her dreams to fall into her lap, she invents them or hunts them down and when she gets the chance to explain that to her mother. Afterwards. Her mother will understand. Understand why she had to do this.

Because her mother has always told her, "Lilac, you aren't an average girl. Not like the others. You're a doer."

And she's right. Here she is. Doing this. She's doing this. Right now.

She checks the map to see if she's still on the right track. Sends Tom a message that she's almost there. Then turns the phone back off. She knows it's basically a tracking device. And she's not ready to be found.

She's almost there.

# Chapter Nine

## SAMANTHA

Day 2

*Sunshine here, in* this region of Washington State, is a special thing. We aren't spoiled with sunshine, so when it comes out, we recognize it for the gift it is.

It feels like the kind of forgiveness I always seem to need. To crave. Not for anything specific. Just for being me. For never being good enough. Guilt. It's an interesting thing in a woman's life. It lingers inside of me in ways I can't fully express. Guilt for things I never had any control over. Yet it's there.

Of course, today when the sun rises I cringe in rebuke of its announcement that today will be a good day. That forgiveness is given. How dare it cascade into my window over the fog, when my eyes are puffy, and my heart is heavy. When, this time, I'm clearly at fault. The air in my house is stale and my breath is musty inside my mouth. I haven't slept and my body is repulsed by the idea that the sun would show itself now.

I'm in so much physical and emotional pain that I take two of my pain meds. They make me even more tired, but I'm used to pushing through it. I'm too wound up to fall asleep. I just sit on the couch, my hands tucked between my thighs. Nowhere to go, no idea what to do. My mind just runs in circles.

The morning rays on the kitchen counter and across the living room floor don't belong. I wrinkle my nose at them accusingly, like they are a lie among many others. This is a moment in time that opens my eyes to all my misconceived notions. Like the world isn't listening or looking at what's happening here. Happening to me. Can't God see that I'm losing my fucking mind?

I can't get ahold of Johnny. I've tried every twenty to thirty minutes for hours. Without purpose or intention. I knew I wouldn't get through to him. I'm turning into the definition of insanity.

I can't get ahold of Lilac either. I've called her fewer times than I've called Johnny. Because I can't reconcile in my mind that she's not available. It scares me every time nobody answers. I prefer denial, honestly. So, I've started calling her less often. Because if I don't call then she can't not answer.

The police have come and gone and told me they'll do everything they can, but to try and embrace the idea that Lilac has run away. That she's "at that age." Whatever that means.

Normal people don't just run away. Not girls with happy lives. Successful lives even.

Not on days where the sun shines. Not on days when the air smells so clean.

I ran away. I ran away because my life was hell. Because everything was all wrong. Because I was assaulted by an older man and used by my mother. I needed to take control of my own life. Of course, my *mother* knew exactly why I had gone. It was a fight and clean break, and it made perfect sense.

But Lilac has everything she could ever want. Doesn't she? Don't we give her everything?

My Lilac doesn't run away. She'd tell me if she was going somewhere. Why wouldn't she? We've always had an open line of communication. She knows just as many of my secrets as I know of hers. It's true we've grown more distant lately, she's so busy with all of her stuff, her growing up and growing famous-ish stuff, and I'm more tired. Taking more medication. More agitated by life and pain. But we're not so distant she'd run away. I can't accept that. It just doesn't make sense. I'm always here for her. A few doors down from her own.

The police said that because her keys are gone, and her car is gone, that she probably left on her own accord. The likelihood that she was kidnapped in her own car without any signs of a struggle was far less plausible than just another teenage adventure, a girl acting out, or one of disobedience, or a mad dash for independence.

They didn't point the finger at me the way I did. But I know they thought it. How could they not think it? If she ran away, she must be running away from something.

When they asked me if she'd been acting out lately, I started to think about the knife incident. I wondered if it had really been a crazy accident. But I didn't mention it to them. Didn't accuse of her of something I didn't know for sure. I didn't want them putting ideas into my head, or vice averse.

They promised they'd check with her school in the morning and her friends, find out where the last place she'd been was. And that made me feel awful. It's awful that my daughter can vanish into thin air, and I don't even know where the place she'd vanished from was exactly. Maybe it was here. Maybe here was the last place anyone had seen her. Maybe it was me and her father. Or maybe not. Maybe she'd been at school like I'd assumed. Maybe she'd gone to her friend Joshua's house.

The police said unless her car turned up, abandoned somewhere, that I shouldn't panic. They said they see this all the time and the teen shows up. Not to worry. They said that it didn't make her a bad kid or mean anything bad about my parenting or our relationship. But I knew.

I knew they were saying that to make me feel better and that it absolutely wasn't true. I knew the truth. That I'm a bad mother now. I'm in the same league as that woman from *Home Alone* that left her son and went on vacation. I have absolutely no idea where my daughter is. And if she did run away. It's probably my fault. I'm not strict enough. Always trying to be her friend.

For a hot minute I wanted to ground her for the rest of her life. And I may still do that if she does show up here unharmed in any way. But like I said, I don't really believe that's the case.

I did check Joshua's house and he said no, he hadn't seen her that day. Teenagers lie. Boys lie. Maybe this is Joshua's fault somehow.

Oh my God. My mind is running now. Running so fast. So willing to blame anyone, or everyone. Not just me, but now I'm targeting her friends.

I stand from the sofa and go to make myself coffee. I haven't slept and I think that maybe I should rest but there's no way I can. I'm watching the clock and waiting for the time I know the school office opens. Because I need to know if she was there yesterday. I need to know exactly how long she was gone before I even knew she was gone.

I pass a mirror on the way to the espresso machine, and I see the mascara and eyeliner streaked down my face. Without even thinking, I pick up a glass vase on the table below the mirror and throw it at the reflection and scream. The shards of glass fly everywhere. Glass from the vase, glass from the mirror. The dog darts off the couch and disappears up the stairs.

I'm so angry. I'm so angry at Johnny. Johnny more than anyone else, because why. Why does he need to be hunting? Why does he need to be so off the grid that I can't even contact him?

I've always told him what if something happens?

What if something happens to me? Or to Lilac. And now look, it did. Of course I was right, but look at him. Gone. Gone just like her. Everyone is gone. And I sink again to my knees because God help me, I must be losing my mind. I have never felt so alone. So helpless.

Lilac would hate to see me this way. She'd call me crazy for breaking the glass. She hates when I lose my temper. She wants me to be more controlled. She'd be ashamed to see me crying on my knees, too. We only believe in strong women in this house. We used to practice kickboxing together when she was younger. Thirteen. Thirteen was one of my favorite ages she's lived through. My RA had just been diagnosed and I was working out to make it better, make myself stronger. I was teaching her self-defense and the importance of being a strong woman.

Now here I am, crying on the floor. Needing somebody else to pick me up because I can't even get up to my feet. Wishing my husband was here to hold me and tell me what to do next. This is truth about how I raised her. I raised her to be better than me. So, if she saw me now, she'd shake her head and maybe laugh. Tell me to toughen up, get my shit together, and go find her.

Because that's what I should be doing right now. Finding her.

The thought drags me back to my feet. Not my own strength, but hers, and her expectations of me.

I skip the coffee and go straight to the shower. I turn on the water to freezing. I step in the ice-cold water and grit my teeth. Goosebumps cover my skin as I shiver in the cold water. There's no space for weakness.

This is exactly what I need. I take a deep breath and count backwards from three. What is it that I *can* do? Not what I want to happen. Not what I'm waiting for to happen. What can I do right now?

When I turn off the water and grab my towel a thought has occurred to me.

I've been checking her social media from my account. Seeing what she's posting to the rest of the world. And it has been completely empty. Totally off brand for her. The comments on the picture of her stitched lip are still going crazy but she hasn't been responding to any of them. Why would a runaway who obsesses over her algorithm moment to moment just stop posting and stop responding to comments? It makes no sense. But maybe there's someplace else to look.

I pick up my phone from the bathroom counter and dial Tanya while my hair drips down my back and with my towel still wrapped around me. Tanya is Johnny's office mate. They are both in technology. Like most people who live here in the suburbs of Seattle. Which is maybe why Johnny feels the need to hunt someplace where technology can't reach him. I don't know. But at least Tanya is here for me. She answers on the second ring.

"Hi, Samantha! What's up, hun?" She calls me hun because on every third Wednesday of the month we all go to happy hour together: her, her husband, Johnny and me. She and I always drink too much and end up deep in gossip and conversation that only drunk women know how to connect in.

I'm thankful now that she has that relationship with me. I'm generally a cold person with few friends. But she likes me. And I'm glad. Because I'm about to ask her to do something that might not fit in with her work ethics code.

"Tanya. I need you to hack Lilac's social media account for me."

I say it so bluntly. But my tired brain has little energy for beating around the bush.

She laughs. Like I told a joke. She doesn't realize I'm serious.

I'm standing there in a windowless bathroom, and I haven't turned on a single light, even in the bathroom, because I'm angry with the light right now. But Tanya can't see that. She doesn't know the state I'm in.

"Um. You know I can't do that, hun. Why? What's up? Is she getting too close with a boy?"

"She's missing, Tanya. Maybe kidnapped."

"Oh my God! Did you call the police?"

"Of course I did! They think she ran away."

"Did she?"

I take a deep breath because this isn't where I wanted our conversation to go. An involuntary shudder runs over my body. Begging for warmth, but I won't give it. Instead, I drop the towel on the floor and walk to my dresser for underwear and an easy sundress.

"Can you come over to my house, please, Tanya? You know Johnny's not here because he's on one of his hunting trips and I'm alone, and I'm freaking out. Please. I need you."

My wet hair dampens the back of the dress immediately. Good. The better to keep me cool, levelheaded, awake with.

"Oh my gosh, yes, I'll be right over."

"Thank you," I say in the most grateful tone I can manage.

And now I can make the coffee.

I'll make two.

Samantha

You need to answer your phone. This is an emergency. Please babe. If you get in a spot where you get any signal at all. Call me immediately. Immediately.

Samantha

Hello?

Samantha

Johnny. Your daughter is missing. She's missing. Gone. Vanished. Call me!!

Samantha

Isn't this what I always said would happen someday? I told you. I. Told. You.

Samantha

God, I'm losing it. I wish you were here.

# Chapter Ten

## LILAC

Night 1

*The dark that* comes with late evening chills Lilac as her headlights creep into Tom's neighborhood. Her car is crawling as she scans the numbers on the houses. Looking for Tom's. A few neighbors peak through their curtains as if she's a prowler and it makes her feel dirty. At least the sky is clear, and the moon provides her a bit of emotional support as she tries to find all her courage.

The darkness of night is different than the

darkness of morning. The darkness of morning provides a promise of daybreak arriving soon. The darkness of night is empty and hollow, with little to offer except cover for wrong doings.

The early morning darkness she left in this morning held all those promises. She drove all day long, and now it's night and dark again. And she doesn't like what this darkness has to offer.

But she's here. Finally, here. Her nerves may be unraveling but she refuses to let them get the best of her. She's not a child afraid of the dark. She reminds herself that this is the moment she's been dreaming about. This will be the story her and Tom tell their grandkids. The story of how they met. She's going to make this moment perfect.

She's heard her mother tell the story of how she met her dad a hundred different times and every time, who it is that's listening smiles with adoration in their eyes, and this right now, this is she and Tom's story. It has to be everything, because after this moment the story is written. It's in stone and they don't get a redo. Even if they tried, the two of them would know it was a lie.

This is pressure. This is their story. Forever.

Her headlights find the number she's been searching for, and Lilac's breath catches in her throat.

The house is small and close to its neighbors. A dingy blue shingled house with a short driveway. The shingles are old and there's a tarp in a place where a few may have been damaged or leaking. Even in the darkness she can tell the house is old and needs to be pressure washed.

The neighborhood doesn't look great by her standards, but she doesn't like to judge people based on their neighborhoods. She knows her mother came from a bad neighborhood in the beginning, then moved to a slightly less bad neighborhood, then moved back to a really bad neighborhood before she met her dad. Her mom has always told her that things like that build character. When she says it, it makes Lilac feel like she's missing out on something by being privileged, like by growing up in a nice neighborhood she can't develop character.

It makes Lilac feel like there's a canyon of knowledge between them. A canyon that she's not allowed to cross.

So, she doesn't judge because she knows she doesn't know what it's like. And she knows from personal experience that things aren't black and white, and she knows her mother is from this side of the privilege canyon.

And Tom, he's only eighteen, of course his house

is small, and he's an entrepreneur like her, so he's still waiting for his business to take off. A skateboarding brand he's building on his social media fame. He hasn't quite reached fame yet, but she believes in him. She knows he will. He has the look. He's hot. And extremely likable. She likes him. So, he must be. It's not like she falls for every hot guy on the internet. Only Tom.

She pulls in the driveway slowly, tires crunching over rocks, headlights reflect back to her from dark windows with curtains drawn. But the porch light is on and that's her sign.

Her heart is truly racing for the first time since she snuck out of her bedroom this morning behind her father. Echoing his footsteps down the hall, so her mother would never have a chance to hear her. Closing the door on her own car as his truck rumbled off into the dark.

Her breath doesn't betray her now, just as it hadn't then. It remains steady, even, her mouth closed. But her fingers are trembling and that makes her laugh to herself. Her nerves are a rare thing. Something that doesn't, and has never, plagued her are nerves.

She's always been happy to be the center of attention. So, these feelings are catching her off guard. But the adrenaline begins to seep in as she puts the car in park, and this is something she knows. This is something she craves. The rush, the intensity of the thrill, not knowing what will happen after the first step off the proverbial mountain. Adrenaline is something she knows well. She clings to that feeling as she walks quickly to the door.

She pushes the button and the ring that echoes through the house makes her stomach drop and she thinks now she needs to pee. Her hands are still shaking so she rubs them together, pretending she's cold. And then he's there. He's opening the door and her lips quiver. She smiles gently with her eyes wide, and he reflects the smile and for a moment they are so bright. Together. Both finally seeing what they've been waiting for all day. All month. All year. The only feeling that surrounds them is electricity and excitement. A thrill and a relief. There he is.

The moment is perfect.

He sweeps her into his arms, and he wraps one arm around her waist and one around her lower back and he presses her whole body against him with his strength. He's very strong. His lips are just as strong, and his tongue reaches deep into her mouth. Over and over again.

She's excited to see him but the aggression in his embrace makes her heart race in a bad way. The pressure feels like it will break through her newly sewn stitches, she winces and tries to pull away. Something feels off. He's too alpha, too aggressive, his tongue is too foreign. She pushes away softly, soft enough that she's embarrassed of it. Flashes of the nurse from yesterday play in her mind. But she doesn't want to ruin this. Only her chest moves back because his arms are still holding on so tightly.

"Whoa," she says as she smiles up at him playfully. "Slow down, I just got here."

"But I've been waiting for you all day," he responds trying again to put his tongue in her mouth.

And this is the first time Lilac questions what exactly she's done. She's cities and state lines away from her home. She's told nobody where she's gone. And now she's inside a man's house that she's never met. And he's looking at her with hungry eyes.

But she knows him, she reminds herself. She wants him to want her. She's seen pictures from him daily on social media. They talk on the phone, and she's messaged the most private things she has to him. It's not like he's a stranger. He's the very thing she wants. He's just excited to see her.

She pulls herself away from him completely and laughs, handing him her bag.

There are conflicting voices in her head, and she needs to silence one of them.

"Okay, well, I'm here now. Where's your bathroom?"

He points her to a door down the small, carpeted hallway, and she smiles at him over her shoulder as she makes her way through it. She presses the flimsy brown with one hand and twists the loose brass handle in her other hand without shaking.

But once she's inside, she locks it behind her. Now her breath does betray her. It comes in a rush and as quickly as she draws it in, it seems to be gone, so she takes another one again. She can't slow it down. She can't make it calm. What the hell is she doing here? What the hell was she thinking? She wants to call her mom, but she knows she can't. Not now. Not like this. Her mom would actually kill her right now. That's not the answer. She has to calm down. Everything's so fine. It's fine.

She looks around her and the bathroom she's standing in is a mess. The tub is yellow behind a scummy curtain and there's grime on the crack where the wall meets the floor. The sink has scum on the ring at the bottom and the handle is spotted with water stains. She cringes when she looks at the thin brown colored towel. It's a boy's bathroom, she tells herself. But that's not really her problem.

Her problem is that Tom looks older than he

does in his pictures. With no filters or ring lights or editing. Or maybe she never really noticed how old he looked, maybe she only registered that he was older than her and didn't stare long enough to try and decided if he was lying about how much older. Yes, she stared. But not at his age. Age isn't a number painted on his six-pack or written across his jaw line. She had just believed him when he said he was eighteen.

But now as she's looking at her baby face in his dirty mirror the conversation is replaying in her head. She'd asked him first, but she'd also answered first.

**How old are you?**

**I'm younger than I look. How old are you?**

**I'm older than I look. Guess how old I am.**

**Hmm. I'm going to guess eighteen.**

**No younger! See. I told you. I'll give you a hint. I'm a sophomore.**

**Oh my God! No you're not.**

He'd made her feel self-conscious about being

young. Made her feel like she needed to prove she was mature enough for him. And in the process, while she was so focused on making him think that she was more mature than her age, she forgot to question whether he was telling the truth about his.

**I am. But I can drive. What year are you?**

**I graduated last year. I live on my own now.**

**Damn. Are you too old for me?**

**I don't know, how old are you?**

**Sixteen.**

**I'm eighteen. Two years.**

**That's not bad. I'm a mature sixteen. Already an established inventor. :)**

**I like that about you. I'm an entrepreneur, too.**

She tries to shake off the feeling. To wipe the

121

conversation from her mind. She must focus on the present. She closes her eyes and opens them. Runs the water as she pees to cover up the sound of her irregular breathing. But now her brain is screaming at her inside her skull, "There's no way that man is eighteen."

She's telling it to shut up. Telling herself that it doesn't matter now. It doesn't even matter how old he is. He's still the same guy he said he was. Everything else is the same.

And besides. Where is she going to go now? What is she supposed to do? Say, sorry, I just realized that I don't believe you're the age you told me, so now I'm going to drive three states back home and we can talk about it over the phone?

No. That's ridiculous.

She's already here. It makes sense that she's nervous. She brushes her bob behind her ear, even though it doesn't stay there. She rinses her mouth by cupping water into her hand to freshen her breath, takes a deep breath and exhales.

As she walks into the living room that clearly belongs to a bachelor, with an old-looking, cheap, black faux-leather couch and a milk crate for a side table, with nothing but a remote on it, he's coming in from the kitchen. The kitchen gives a yellow glow at his back, and it makes the color of his skin look sour. No wonder he only takes pictures at the skate park.

He's carrying two drinks and he hands one to her. It's bubbly.

"Champagne, to celebrate us finally being together."

Lilac smiles, but this time it's only politely. She's sixteen. She might be a lot of things, and she might have done a lot of things, but Lilac doesn't drink. She knows exactly how alcohol affects the brain and she values her inhibitions. A hunter knows better. A hunter's daughter has been trained better. Sharpness is the difference between life and death, and she doesn't like to be caught off her guard. She's not dumb and she's seen all the trending videos from victimized women. Drunk girls turn into raped girls.

She's also seen firsthand what happens to people when they drink, and she knows the second a girl drinks she's more like prey than what Lilac ever wants to be. She clinks the glass with Tom's and she presses it to her lips, but she doesn't drink. She doesn't even sip. Now is when her honed and trained, keen senses kick in.

It's her heritage.

Samantha

**Lilac?**

Samantha

**I'm worried about you. Please call me if you get this.**

Samantha

**I called the police. We're looking for you. If you're in trouble, we'll find you. I promise.**

Samantha

**If someone else is getting these texts, do not hurt my daughter. I will find you and I will kill you!**

# Chapter Eleven

## SAMANTHA

Day 2

*I place the* cup of coffee I made for Tanya into her hands the minute she walks in the door. She's a round busty woman who dresses like a fashionable school principal. Tight shirts tucked into long skirts with thick belts and flower print. Everything always matches. Her dark brown curls are always bouncy and the rims on her glasses are always thick but a different color every time I see her. Today they are violet.

"I called the school. Lilac wasn't there yesterday. They said they had left a message on my voicemail, and I'm an idiot because I never even checked it. I never check my voicemail."

The words coming out of my mouth are rushed, I'm on my third cup of coffee since I called Tanya. I had to warm hers up in the microwave.

There are tears in my eyes and I know Tanya sees them. Even if they haven't escaped to my cheeks yet. It's just a matter of time and her and I both know it.

"It's okay, hun, sit down. Nobody checks their voicemail. You aren't the only one."

The house is chaos and I know it. There's glass everywhere. Somehow our family picture got knocked crooked. There are fingerprints on the glass of a photo of Lilac I spent a few hours staring at last night.

Tanya's hand is caring on my back as she walks me into the living room and steers me toward the couch. She doesn't mention the sticky dried dog pee on the floor, but I know she sees it because she steps around it. I had forgotten about it until she did that. After she makes sure I'm seated she sets her cup down and navigates the glass on the floor through the kitchen to get paper towels. She knows we keep the spray bottle under the sink, and she grabs that, too.

"She's been missing since yesterday morning!

She's been gone for a full twenty-four hours! I need your help, Tanya, please."

It's harder for her to say no to me now that she's looking at me in the face. Now that she's looking at the state of my house and the emptiness of my environment. An environment that usually has a loving couple and a mouthy teenager. Even the dog is out of sight, laying in Lilac's bed. She knows something is wrong, too.

Inside this house, Tanya really feels the situation I'm in now. My husband being unreachable for the next week and my daughter missing.

So she doesn't say no, and that's a small victory for me.

After she cleans the dog mess on the floor, she sits down on the couch that's across from me, holding her cup of coffee between her two hands, her eyes diverting from the broken glass still on the kitchen floor. I haven't even tried to clean it up. I'll get to it. But it's not priority. Finding my daughter is priority. And I'm glad that Tanya realized that, too, and left it.

"Samantha, what is the last thing you remember? Did you two have a fight? Does she have a reason to run away?"

"No!" I yell and it's from exhaustion. I wouldn't have yelled if I wasn't so tired. It was a bad play on my part and Tanya is taken aback. Her eyes stray back to the mirror and vase comingled on the floor.

"I'm sorry," I say, and lower my voice to something quieter than before, something to counterbalance the yell, bring us back to center. "It's just that I don't understand why everyone keeps suggesting she's run away. She would never do that."

"Well," Tanya is looking at the carpet under her feet as she's speaking and I can tell she's trying to choose her words carefully, "The thing is, Lilac is a little crazy sometimes, not crazy, but bold. Bold is a better word. And Samantha, her car isn't here."

She says the last sentence delicately, trying hard to keep me calm, so I put effort into presenting that way. Even though inside I'm fuming. Lilac isn't crazy. She's exceptional.

"If she had ran away, why didn't she leave a note?"

"She's mad at you?"

I bite my lip hard enough to force the tears from my eyes and out onto my cheeks. And once the floodgates are open, they don't stop. I'm losing ground with Tanya, and I know that she may be right. In fact, I'm starting to hope she is right, and that the police are right, that maybe Lilac just ran away. Because if she really has been missing for over twenty-four hours and nobody has done anything to help me, well then, I can't say how this might end. I can't say what might have happened to her. At least if she ran away, I could hope she's fine. Or that she'll be back soon.

"I'm just so scared, Tanya. She's only sixteen. Even if she did run away, she's the perfect age to be picked up by human traffickers."

Tanya's eyes flicker then and I see she's coming around to my level of anxiety. I push harder.

"What if she ran away to meet a boy she met online, and he kidnaps her and rapes her. She's famous, you know. She gets messages from boys all the time and I'm constantly trying to warn her, but some of them are really good, some of them are really convincing."

And then I remember. I remember how the night before she went missing, when we were riding in the car, home from the hospital, she wasn't even looking at me. She was typing on her phone. Obsessively. She said she was answering all the comments on her photo, but she wasn't.

"Oh my God," I say out loud. Coffee sloshes out of my cup as I set it down on the coffee table a little too hard. I don't even bother to get up and get a napkin or wipe it up. My mind is racing.

"What?" Tanya sounds just as worried as me now. She sets her coffee cup down, too, though more gently than I did. Hers stays inside of her cup.

"I'm right. I'm right." I look directly at her. "It's a boy. She was messaging a boy. Come on, let's go to the computer. I *need* your help."

And this time when I stand up, Tanya doesn't protest or try to convince me that I need to sit, she just follows me silently into the home office. We both know that if a boy is involved in this crazy disappearing act, Lilac could be in trouble and not even know it.

In little less than an hour Tanya has provided me access to all of Lilac's social media accounts. She really is good at her job.

The two of us are sitting at the oversized wooden desk with a walnut finish. She's in the leather office chair and I'm on a kitchen chair. We've been sliding the keyboard back and forth and right now it's in front of me.

Lilac doesn't answer most of her direct messages, so it isn't hard to find the messages between her and some guy named Tom. It's the only extremely active DMs.

Tanya's face is pale and expressionless. Mine is hot with anger and embarrassment.

He asked her to come visit and then she told him she would, but then he asked her to move to text because he doesn't feel comfortable sharing his address over the internet. Which I find highly amusing, but even more frustrating, considering the horrifying pictures these two have been sending.

There are so many pictures of Lilac in and out of her underwear. It's such a strong contrast to the framed photo of her in braided pigtails on the desk. It makes me want to vomit and scream all at the same time. I wish she were here so I could warn her how dangerous it is to put things like this on the internet. These pictures are out there now and she can never take them back. There's always ways these things leak. Things teenage girls never think about. They think they can trust that their account will never get hacked or his account will never get hacked. But worse, they trust the boy that they're sending them to will never change his feelings about her. And that's just not the way life works. If they ever fight. They're leaked. If they break up, they're leaked, or sold, especially in an influencer's case.

But Lilac isn't here to have that conversation with. I'm already too late. It makes me mad at myself. I should have known she was doing this. How did I not know? I slide the keyboard back over to Tanya in disgust.

"I can't look anymore."

She takes the mouse and clicks out of the DMs.

"Neither can I."

Tanya scrolls through Tom's page, and we start stalking it. Reading every caption. Looking at every picture. Browsing all the comments.

Tom has told my daughter that he's eighteen, but a mother isn't stupid. I was, however, stupid before I became a mother and that makes me even better at spotting his obvious lie. Tom is clearly in his twenties. There's not even a doubt in my mind. And the fact that he's made my sixteen-year-old daughter travel across the country to see him? Well, let's just say he's lucky my husband isn't home. Yet.

Tom's going to be lucky to make it out of all this alive. That's how I feel now at least. My blood is boiling watching as Tanya browses his page. Seeing his pictures without shirts, doing skateboarding tricks, and smiling that shit-eating grin.

The comments are all from girls who are fawning over him. I want to take him by the throat and pluck out his stupid beady eyeballs.

"Tanya, can you get me into his account?"

"Sure," she says. She doesn't even hesitate. She clearly feels the same way as me about this greasy haired creep of a man.

"What kind of adult man preys on young girls like this?"

When she says it, I shudder. I shudder because I know the answer to that question. I know what kind of man. I've been there and done that, but there is no way that Tanya knows this when she says what she says, so I don't respond. She doesn't know my past. And I'll keep it like that. But the blood that's boiling under my skin right now is harder to hide.

I push the kitchen chair back so I can stand. I can pace around a bit.

"A bad kind of man," I answer. It's all I can say.

Tom's private messages look nothing like Lilac's. His are very active. He's been messaging at least a hundred girls. All the same gross bullshit, it feels personal, it is personal, and now my fingernails are digging into my thighs through my yoga pants and I'm trying not to scream.

There's sext thread after sext thread and my stomach is sinking as Tanya is trying to find Samantha's thread.

"Maybe she deleted something. Maybe the address is on his side."

We both know it's a long shot when Tanya says it but it's all we can hope for right now. We need something. We need a break.

"Or maybe he's added his address to one of these other threads?"

But I can't go on. I can't keep looking at this betrayal. This predator that convinced my child she found love.

I want to vomit. Instead, I stand up and I scream.

I punch the wall and the drywall gives under my fist, then I cry, leaning my head onto my throbbing hand.

"How did this happen?" I say to myself, but Tanya thinks I'm talking to her, so she answers.

"Social media is just so dangerous for kids."

And that kind of breaks me inside because it's what I've said from the beginning, but I kept giving in and I kept giving in, because it seemed unavoidable at a certain point. And then I became complacent and accepting. I let my daughter rise to 1.2 million followers because I thought it was her destiny and out of my control, and now even flipping Doby has an account.

My hand hurts so bad, I turn to search the room for a bottle of my Oxy, but it's not here, the only one I have right now is still upstairs.

I grab the lamp from the table, and I throw it. The ceramic base shatters when it hits the wall.

Tanya looks at her phone and says, "Oh, I have to go."

I guess this has become too much for her. It's become too much for me.

She looks at me as she rolls the chair back and stands, smoothing her long skirt.

"Samantha, I'm so sorry."

"No," I say holding my hand over my nose. Trying to hold back all the emotions that are threatening to explode from inside me. Trying to cope with the crushing pain in my chest and my body. "You should go."

# Chapter Twelve

## LILAC

Night 1

*Lilac grips her* steering wheel because she knows that she's in over her head, accidentally. Like jumping off a cliff into the ocean on vacation. A cliff you were coaxed into getting on top of, one that you jumped from because you craved the adrenaline, you just wanted to prove you could. To yourself and to anyone else in the world that may ever question your ability to jump. But then you hit the ocean and it's nothing like you expected. It's stronger. Violent. But you're already in and now you have no choice but to fight it. You're in it, and now you have to find your way back to the shore or die.

That's exactly how Lilac feels now. Sick to her stomach but focused, ready to survive.

She's already jumped.

She had to get out of that house though. She couldn't stay there any longer. She couldn't risk more unknowns on Tom's turf. Now she's in her car and cruising this small town.

How many people here know Tom? The suburb looks similar in size to hers and she runs into people she knows everywhere at home. She literally can't leave hers without running into someone she knows. She's probably surrounded by people that know Tom.

She looks to her left and her right and the street feels smaller. The houses feel closer. There are not enough stores. She's always been prone to claustrophobia, so she recognizes it now.

She pulls into the parking lot of a hardware store and drives slowly by the front door. The lights are still on. There are hardly any cars, but it's late. She parks and tries to slow her breathing.

She thinks of her father. What he's doing right now. Thinks of the way he's perfectly still in his stand in the trees. He forces his heart not to quicken when he sees his prey, he says they can hear your heartbeat if it races. She thinks of the way he moves. Deliberately. She channels him now as she steps out of her car. Slides her keys between her fingers.

She's in charge. She's not prey. She's the hunter.

She tells herself these things in her mind over and over. Like a mantra.

She's in charge. She's not prey. She's the hunter.

One look over her shoulder as she walks inside, just to check her car in the dark, and then she steps through the automatic sliding doors. The lights are bright and something about the smell of the wood and the tools, it strikes a feeling of safety inside her. Even a hundred miles from home, hardware smells the same. Like trees. Like the forest. Like her father. She'd stay here all night if she could. If the store didn't close soon.

What would her father buy? What are the things she needs to keep her safe? To keep her on top. Top of the food chain.

"Good evening, ma'am. Kind of late for a young lady like yourself to be in here alone, isn't it? You picking up something for your father?"

An older gentleman in a vest with a nametag doesn't mean to offend her. But it doesn't change the fact that he does. Lilac's eyes narrow, and she feels more again like herself.

She smiles. The man doesn't realize her teeth are those of the wolf.

"Yes, actually I am. Thank you."

"What's he need? I'll help you."

"Ummm," she rolls her eyes up to the ceiling, trying to channel the things her father would buy if he were in her shoes right now. Then she looks down at the ground. No, those things would never do. Her father has taught her a lot. A lot about observation, about stillness, about waiting and patience for the right moment to strike. About murder. But he underestimates the beast in men. Lilac knows better because she was born a woman. She's always been assumed to be prey, so she knows that men with a certain look in their eye assumes to be her predator.

She knew that look as soon as she was sitting there on the couch next to Tom.

"I need rope and a knife. Like you know, he needs something to cut the rope with," she clarifies before he starts questioning things.

"He's building my little brother a tree house. Sweet, huh? The rope is really for aesthetics."

The man nods and turns, expecting her to follow.

"Oh, and cigarettes and a lighter."

The man looks over his shoulder as she adds,

"For my father, obviously."

His gray hair nods and she shrugs. She's never smoked before. But she's watched Joshua, her closest friend in the world, do it almost every day for the past year. He started when his anxiety levels spiked after his parents' divorce, and he said it helped. Said it calmed him down. And since she could certainly use anything that may calm her down now, she has the urge. She'll follow it. Just to see.

The gentleman leads her to rope and then to box cutters.

"These will work to cut the rope," he says as he hands her a heavy-duty box cutter.

She takes them both without speaking. She's done with small talk. She focuses now. Intensely.

The older man checks her out personally and even though he hesitates to give her the cigarettes after she tells him she forgot her ID. She reminds him they're for her dad anyways and he winks sliding them in and typing in information from his own ID.

She forces the sweetest smile she can muster. And then she leaves.

His eyes burn at her back, she knows he's still watching, can feel his appraising eyes. So she decides to give him a show, stops outside the front door, peels the plastic from the carton of cigarettes and then the aluminum, the way she's watched Joshua do a hundred times.

She slides the first one out, pulls the lighter from the plastic bag and takes her first drag. When her eyes meet the man's eyes through the glass door, he's scowling. His eyebrows pinching together in a deep crease. She smiles, a real smile this time, thrilled at his disapproval, and she waves as she turns and heads back to her car.

The smell of the tobacco in her fingers reminds her of Joshua. He was right about it calming her down. It's like magic. Almost too good. No wonder it's addicting. The richness of it takes her back to his room and she wishes he was here. He'd know what to do. Probably.

She thinks about it only long enough to play it out in her head. Turning on her phone. Calling him. Her mom going over there and grilling him. No. She can't put Joshua in that position. Even if she's confident he'd lie for her. He shouldn't have to lie for her. That's not what friends do to each other.

So instead, she gets in the car and starts to drive. Drives out into the dark. She's not sure where she's going, but she's done with the tight streets and all the buildings. All their windows. Watching her.

She heads for the road that leads her back out of

town.

Samantha

By the way, I know we've chosen to raise our
child without violence. But there's a good chance
I beat her once I find her.

# Chapter Thirteen

### SAMANTHA

Day 2

*The intrusive blue* rays from the computer screen and the strain in my eyes are making my head ache near the top of my skull. The coffee, Oxy, and emptiness in my gut are making my blood sugar feel off. I know I need to take a break from the screens and make myself something to eat, take some ibuprofen, but my hyper focused personality trait has taken over and I can't tear myself away from the screen.

The white glow of the screen in my otherwise yellow office is sucking me in like I've been put in a hypnotic trance.

I've been going through Tom's social media and DM's obsessively for hours now. I'm certain that the answer to finding my daughter is here. I know that she's with him. This exact person who has made this profile and messaged all these girls is the same man who has messaged and manipulated mine. The problem is, the person he says he is on this page, doesn't exist.

I've already ran the background check on three different "people finder" websites. They all said the same thing, there is no eighteen-year-old Tom Dillinger that lives in Utah. Of course, I already knew he was lying about his age. That was obvious. So, I tried many different age options. Every one of them in fact, from eighteen to thirty. Nothing.

I've also tried copying and pasting his photos into Google to see if they show up somewhere else under a different name, but they don't. They seem to really be his pictures. Even if they are heavily edited. They aren't from some stock photo website or from some model agency or porn site. He appears to be this guy. And he doesn't appear to be all over the internet. Just in this one place.

And now, after hours of reading his manipulative

speech pattern he's been targeting at hundreds of teenage girls and seeing his disgusting pictures and their vulnerable ones that would probably devastate them if they leaked into the public domain, I hate Tom. I hate him more than I've ever hated any man in my life. And I've hated quite a few men.

I've hated less than quite a few, but more than a couple men particularly aggressively, and obsessively.

Tom has just topped that list, however.

I never hated any man as much as this.

There's something about the kind of love that a mother has for her daughter, and the deep desire to protect her from the ruthless nature of unsavory type men. From the damage that she knows herself. This kind of love can make hate grow roots deeper than what's healthy or manageable.

The hate that this man's actions and words and pictures are watering inside of me is quickly turning into an invasive type of weed. There's little chance of fully removing it.

There's one girl who is fifteen that he's been messaging every day. She sends him pictures of her in the shower in bathing suits. She still has baby cheeks, and it takes me thirty minutes to track down her mother on a different site and open a new profile under a fake name so I can send her mother one of the pictures and let her know her daughter is messing with strangers on the internet. I do it because I wish someone had done it for me. I want to message all these girl's mothers. And maybe if my own daughter wasn't missing. If I wasn't losing valuable time every minute I waste worrying about every other girl in Tom's DMs, then I probably would track down all their mothers. But the fact is that I don't have that kind of time.

I heard once that if you don't find a missing child within the first forty-eight hours then the chances of finding that child alive drops drastically. I don't know if that statistic applies to teenage girls that have run away. Or how human trafficking plays into that statistic. But I know that I'm too close to that forty-eight-hour mark to do the research.

No. I'm missing something. I must be. My eyes are burning from staring at the computer screen. They're dry around the edges, and they burn from the tears that have seeped into the dry cracks. I rub my hands over them and let them rest, close them with my elbows on the desk and try to make my mind stop racing.

I should really stumble into the kitchen and get that ibuprofen.

Why hasn't she called me? Why didn't she leave me a note? Has it not even crossed her mind that I'm dying inside right now? Maybe he's taken her phone. Maybe he has her tied up and shot up with drugs in her veins already. My smart, sassy girl, with all her success, couldn't be saved from this world full of dark men.

My thoughts are spiraling, and I know I'm making assumptions, and trying to slow my thoughts doesn't seem to be working so I stand and begin to pace. I walk to the living room and grab my phone that's been sitting on the coffee table. The screen is hauntingly blank. No calls. No calls from Lilac. No texts. No messages from Johnny. Nothing from the police.

I click into my social media from my screen name to check if there's anything new to Lilac's account.

My heart races and then it sinks. I don't know if the picture even warrants relief or what it means. A new picture uploaded this morning but obviously taken last night. She must have posted it while I was logged in to Tom's account, obsessively studying his DMs.

A dark sky rolling into the last rays of the day. I imagine a dark song with low chords playing too loud on her radio. The picture is taken from behind the steering wheel, through the front windshield.

Its caption reads: Road trip! Will be gone for a few days! Love and miss you, Mom!

When I read the last word Mom, my walls break and my chest heaves. I ugly cry immediately and I sink down onto the couch. The phone slowly slides from my fingertips and thuds onto the ground, and I soak the throw pillow under my face.

I cry so hard for so long, until no more tears can come from my body. I'm empty. And then I finally. Finally. Sleep. It takes me over; I don't give into it. But it wins. I've exhausted everything inside of me. And as I drift off the last thing that I think is: I'm going to find Tom. And when I do, he's going to know a mother's wrath like he's never imagined. I imagine that he's never even given it a thought. All the girls he's been screwing with, and he's probably never even imagined what their mothers would do to him. I am married to a murderer after all. I married him because I loved him. I certainly have it in me.

Samantha

I found a guy that Lilac has been talking to, but he's lying to her. About a lot. I think she's gone to see him.

Samantha

I hate him. Johnny. I actually hate him.

Samantha

...

# Chapter Fourteen

## LILAC

Day 2

*The sun rises* over Utah in a way that feels ancient. Like it's been doing it just the same for millions of years, and the land is expecting it. The land feels like an ancient thing out here, too. Away from the towns and the cities. Lilac's happy she drove so far last night.

Gentle rays of warmth reach down to her soul, even as the morning air blows crisp against her skin. All the terror and anxiousness of the dark fades away with the sunrise. This is what small blessings feel like. Like the sunrise after a particularly intense and grueling night. It feels like a message from the heavens. A nod of acceptance and approval. A sign that the world is at her back with a hand on her shoulder.

She's leaned up against her car with her face to the sky and her eyes closed. Not even worried about the dirt and dust that's accumulated on the paint and now rubs off onto her clothing. She slept for only three hours in the driver's seat and yet there is no desire to sleep more at the edges of her brain. Teenagers are trained for these kinds of things.

Life feels long when you're young, but still Lilac knows youth doesn't last. These days that feel like forever will be gone before she knows it. Her mother tells her that. So, she takes a deep breath and reminds herself to enjoy every adventure like it could be her last. This one has felt a little more like it may be her last than most.

When she looks around her, she sees nothing but landscape and the dirt road she found last night in the dark, by luck, illuminated in her headlights. Utah is such a beautiful place. The color of rich dirt. And distant rock formations. The flat land between her and them is speckled with small green plants. The abandoned barn that is falling apart beside her car seems out of place.

Forgotten because it was misplaced. It's nothing like her suburb is outside of Seattle. Where the green is large and looming. Where trees dominate the people and their buildings, and the rain and moss and mold make the working barns look abandoned when they're not. No. This barn is forgotten.

Abandonment being more than a facade, and in fact an actuality. It reminds her of her mother. Her mother is always talking about her abandonment issues. Lilac wonders if this barn struggles with any of the same issues. If the walls could talk, would they tell her to stay away for fear that they may grow accustomed to her, only for her to leave them, too.

If they could talk and did say such a thing, they'd be right. But that isn't going to keep her from loving it now. Good thing it's just a barn.

The dust is thick and undisturbed. The sun has long ago faded the paint.

After a deep, invigorating breath that fills her lungs and calms her mind she walks over to the barn. The door is already cracked far enough for her to slip in. She left it that way.

On a thick wooden beam that runs from the ceiling to the floor in the middle she sees that Tom is still asleep.

It was a pain in the ass getting him in there.

Drugged out of his mind, he was dead weight in her arms. Luckily Lilac is strong.

Again, that's thanks to her mom. Always pushing her. Always training her to be something more than what she already is. Kickboxing lesson after kickboxing lesson. Grueling routine that's lead to a level of strength she didn't even quite realize she had. She knew she was strong, of course. But never took it here in her mind, not this.

Lilac never knows what her mother's training her for, but maybe it is this. Maybe her mother knew one day Lilac would face a man like this.

He looks so uncomfortable; she can't imagine how sore he will be when he wakes up. His arms behind him, around the splintering beam. Small pieces of wood stuck in his skin. And his wrists tied with rope behind him. His neck is bent funny and his head hangs limp with the curls of his hair falling in his face.

Lucky for him, she had found an old wooden chair to place him on. His ankles are tied to the legs and his feet reach the floor.

Unlucky for him, the chair seemed to be infested with spider eggs under the seat and a few parents in their webs. Maybe his luck will change. Maybe they'll stay put, just the way they are, for the duration of their stay. Lilac knows that's a risk she wouldn't want to take herself. But maybe he's one of those big bad boys that aren't afraid of spiders. Or maybe he's the kind that has smashed so many and laughed at their dead bodies because they made him feel bigger. Stronger. And now. Perhaps this is his karma.

Doesn't matter though. He's tied tightly to this chair. And so far, he's still out cold.

She stands in front of him. Keeping her distance. At least six feet away. Slim rays of the sun that have made their way through the cracks between the planks of wood on the barn fall across his face. The dust in the air floats gracefully between them.

She marvels at the fact that he hasn't woken. She's dragged him to her car. He's ridden in her trunk for hours. And she's dragged and tied him in this barn. Drugs like this one really shouldn't be around. Or at least, people should be more aware of them. Educated on them.

Given tools in school on how to avoid them, and what to do if one comes across them.

She thinks back to the drugs she was warned about in school. In the programs where police came to the class and kids whispered about the things you aren't supposed to do. She remembers weed. Pot was a big one. Things you smoked. Or took because they were offered to you. Because you were a bad kid, and you were trying to have the bad kind of fun. The kind of fun that killed you.

There were vapes and pills that were supposed to make you feel high, but nobody ever talked about this.

A drug that a man may try to sneak you, so you would black out cold, and then he could do whatever the fuck he wanted to you.

Only her mother. Her mother had warned her about this.

The kind of drugs men gave to women when they weren't looking.

The kind that erased their memory and blacked them out like they were dead, so men could do whatever they liked to those unsuspecting women. Anything at all. Rape, beat, kill, kidnap, torture. Lilac had always thought her mom was obnoxiously over-concerned about things that she would never really have to worry about.

Her dad always rolled his eyes and told Lilac to ignore her. They'd both laughed at the extremeness of the things she would say. It seemed so unbelievable. So unlikely. If it was really that likely, why wouldn't she learn about it in school. Why wouldn't someone else prepare her for this. Why wouldn't her dad take it seriously, too?

She had thought it nonsense. A nothing to worry

about scenario.

She had been wrong.

Thank God her mother had taught her about these.

She pulls her phone out of her back pocket and walks out of the barn, trying to find a signal.

She walks down the dirt road for a mile and a half, closer to the main road she turned from in the night.

When she finally sees a signal, she posts a picture she took last night. She has over a million followers but the only person she's thinking of when she posts the picture of the night taking over the day from the previous evening, is her mom.

"Thank you, Mom," she whispers. Then turns around and heads back to the barn.

THE VEGETARIAN AND HER HUNTER

Samantha

I don't want to alarm you more than I already have. But I feel like this guy could be into human trafficking.

158

# Chapter Fifteen

## SAMANTHA

Day 2

*I wake on* the couch with my cheek hot and wrinkled from the pressure on the throw pillow. My head is heavy with the kind of sleep that throws you deep into REM as soon as you give up on staying awake. But thank God the headache is gone.

The room is bright with the light of full day. The soft white curtains contrast against the gloom of my eye bags. Doby is back by my side and licking my face.

I wake up sore and stiff and groan because my pain meds are upstairs, and the couch hasn't been nice to my body. But I'm alive and I believe Lilac is alive now, too, so that's something. I have the strange sensation that none of this can be real, that I've somehow been catapulted into some f'd up alternate reality. The thing about life though, is it's filled with these little moments where it feels like the floor shouldn't be there under your feet. Like someone has ripped it out from underneath of you. And yet, you're still standing.

When I was a child, I always felt that way. It was something I expected. It was the days where the floor felt solid that I stood the most carefully, braced myself for the moment that would inevitably come. The moment someone would rip my security away from under me. That's what happens when you're taken from your first home, first family, and then given to a new family. When you believe that family is stable and you define them in your mind as such, and then your father disappears, and your mother resents you. When you used to love each other and then you don't. And shit just rolls downhill like a snowball from there. You get used to the floor tilting and changing what the definition of reality is.

I guess I've grown complacent and comfortable

over these years I've spent with Johnny. Happy. Trusting. Something I never thought I'd say. I stopped standing with my heart braced for a fall. So, this whole thing has thrown me for a loop. But it's not like I've never been in a loop before. So now that I'm rested, I'm remembering how to stand without the floor underneath me.

It still takes me a minute of groggy staring around at nothing, as I walk to the fridge and grab a yogurt, to fully remember the situation I'm in.

The situation we're in. Lilac and myself. My husband doesn't even know he's in a situation. Even though I've been texting him a play by play, I know he's not getting my texts. He won't get them until he's back in a place where he can get service. How nice that must be right now for him. Blissfully ignorant.

But I feel calmer. Not as close to the edge of something, like I did before reading Lilac's post, and before I finally fell asleep. The desperation and chaos that was consuming me has fizzled into a methodical thing that's organizing my thoughts as quickly as I remember them. I spoon strawberry yogurt into my mouth as I think.

The phone company is the first thing my thoughts land on that feels like a call to action.

I haven't tried the phone company. I want to kick

myself for not thinking of it sooner.

I've always respected Lilac's privacy, and now I see that possibly that was a mistake.

But in this moment, I'm grateful that at least we are on the same phone plan.

It's been a long time since I've heard the phone company keeps track of all the texts sent and received on any device on any plan, but I feel certain that they still do it.

Data is more valuable than anything else in our society. That's something Johnny's always saying. He and his tech friends.

I pick my phone up off the ground and stare at it. I don't get bills; those are paperless now. I go into the phone store when I have a problem with my phone. But they aren't our service provider.

I search the internet for our service provider and call the number I find for customer support. These are things Johnny usually handles. Phone things.

After a few transfers and some long-winded explanations, a woman finally informs me that the information I'm looking for is being sent to my inbox.

My finger swipes over to my inbox and I refresh until I see the new message. It's exactly what the lady promised. The text history of Lilac's phone.

Thank God for data that never dies. This time.

It only takes me moments to find where the social media messages stopped, and direct text messages began.

Just like that, I have an address.

I'm grabbing the keys and my purse and running to my car as I dial Tanya's number. It switches over to Bluetooth as I start the car and she answers sounding tired.

"Hey, Samantha, any news?"

"I'm going on a road trip. Come by and take care of the dog tonight, will you?"

"Yes, of course. You find her?"

"Let's just say I'm going on a hunting trip."

Tanya laughs nervously, but she knows not to ask questions.

"Aren't you the vegetarian?"

Tanya's weak joke falls flat as I don't respond, she and I both know how I feel about animals doesn't change how I feel about this man who has convinced my child to wander outside the safety of my arms and beyond my reach. We both know.

"Of course, hun, I'll watch the dog. You do what you gotta do," she tries again.

"Thanks, girl."

I'm lucky to have a friend like Tanya.

"Good luck, hun."

After I hang up, I turn the car around and pull back in the drive. The safe is upstairs and it's been a while since I've tried to use it, but I'm not rusty. I guess some things are like riding a bike. My gun is light and small and slides into my purse easily.

"Okay," I say as I adjust the rearview mirror and look at myself in the eyes, "Now, I'm going hunting."

The stick in the middle slides to reverse and I back out.

"Good luck, Tom."

I hit the gas and drive.

"But not really."

Samantha

FYI - don't worry if you get all these messages and then race home and nobody's there. I found an address for the guy. I'm going to get Lilac.

Samantha

We'll probably be back before you.

# Chapter Sixteen

**LILAC**

Day 2

*The walk back* to the barn feels shorter than the walk away from it. Space is strange that way. It always takes more effort to walk away than to walk back. When Lilac returns, she's greeted with the noise of a struggle inside the barn. The sound of huffing and puffing and scraping of wood on the barn floor quickens the pace of her heartbeat and she stops to steady her breath before she slips in.

He doesn't see her at first because her steps are light, her footing is soft. She's purposefully quiet as she stands by the door and watches the confusion on his face, the manic panic as he twists and turns in the ropes she's tied.

But she's a good little girl and learned all the lessons about rope tying her father had to teach. Tom isn't going anywhere. It's a strange sort of pleasure she feels watching him struggle. Like she's getting an A on a term paper. Like all the lessons she'd learned weren't for nothing. Her father would be so proud.

She clears her throat as she steps into a light beam from one window in the top of the barn. She didn't plan to be dramatic, but she kind of likes the effect it has. Like she's stepped on a stage. She's always fancied herself the actress type. Likes the idea of attention.

Tom freezes and looks up. His eyes widen and his smile quakes on one side, she's caught him off guard. It appears like he didn't expect her to be the one standing there.

"Lilac? Hi."

He's trying for charm and that amuses her because he couldn't be charming if he pleaded for marriage in this moment. If he promised her a life of leisure, flowers, and diamonds. If he took that stupid smile and straight teeth and started quoting Shakespeare or poetry. Tom will never seem charming again.

"Oh, Tom. Let's not pretend to be friends right now. You tried to drug me, and I've got you tied up in a barn. We aren't doing so well together, are we?"

She laughs at herself and decides to push the joke further.

"Maybe we should have taken one of those love match quizzes before I drove all the way down here."

She pretends to point at an imaginary sentence in the air with her finger.

"Do you like to be drugged without consent? Yes? You might be a match. No?" She draws a check with her hand, "Turn back now."

She sees that his face clears, and his confusion is vanishing before her eyes, but he doesn't try to drop the charming act. He commits. Gives it his all.

"Lilac. What are you talking about? I didn't try to drug you. Why would you say that?"

He laughs like his innocence is pure and he would never do anything so absurd. It humors her a little, but not as much as it angers her.

She doesn't bother laughing now, because if she did, she'd sound like a maniac. It would be completely forced. Tom killed any humor that existed in the vibe.

She steps closer, her anger feeding her bravery. The light is at her back now and the shadows dance over her face. The early morning light that had shone across his is gone.

"Tom. When you went to the bathroom after me, I switched our drinks. Can you remember last night? Or no. I'm not sure exactly how the effects of this drug work."

Her eyes roll and she wants to scream at her own stupidity for ever liking this man. Instead she reflects this anger at him.

"How stupid can you be? You put a drug in my drink and then left yours unattended. Did you really not have even the slightest concern that I'd switch our drinks? You thought there was a zero percent chance I'd do that? You must think I'm completely incapable of any kind of self-preservation."

He stares at her blankly, the smile on his face drooping.

"I," he stutters out and then tries again, "I don't know what you're talking about."

"Oh, come on. You do. I know you do. Think hard."

The hairs on the back of her neck prickle as she gets closer to him. The adrenaline releasing into her veins as she gets close enough to touch him, she wants to touch him. She wonders how strong he really is. If he got angry enough, and clever enough, could he break the wood he was tied to?

"I saw your face, love. I saw how disappointed you were that my drink was still so full in my hand when you came back. And so, you chugged yours, hoping I'd follow your lead."

Lilac can't hold herself back from the cliff in front of her. He's so pretty and so evil. She's filled with hate, anger, and a need to make him feel the emotions he's shoved down her throat. Leading her on for months, making her think they were soul mates, perfect for each other. Only to try and take her free will from her the moment she walked through his door. She had trusted him! Cared for him.

The fire in her chest is telling her to do the same thing to him. But there is no way to give him back what he gave her. There's no turning around or starting over. She trusted him and he used that trust as if it were naivety. She may never be able to trust again. He's broken her ability to trust. She wants him to pay. She wants him to feel her pain.

She reaches out her hand and places it under his chin. He jerks his head back and turns his face away like he's startled by her touch. Like he didn't expect her to cross that line. Even though he clearly intended to with her.

"Oh, what, Tom? You don't think it's okay to

touch somebody when they have no capacity to stop you?"

"Lilac, stop." Tom laughs and his laugh sounds a bit crazed. "You're being crazy. Just let me up. Let's get out of here."

"I'm crazy?"

Lilac laughs.

"You don't even know me, Tom. You don't even know what I'm capable of. You don't know what crazy is yet, Tom," she emphasizes yet and she emphasizes his name, she has no intention of letting him go, and every intention of making him pay. He needs to learn a lesson.

She just needs to figure out how to teach it.

She smacks him hard across the face. Hard enough to leave her own hand feeling like fire. She turns to walk back toward the door and relishes in the sound of his voice as he says her name. Pleads for her to come back. Back down from the crazed place in her mind to which he's lead her. But she has no intention of turning around.

He can wait.

Samantha

**The cash in my wallet is gone. I guess Lilac must have taken it. So… it's official, runaway she is then.**

# Chapter Seventeen

## SAMANTHA

Night 2

*The darkness arrived* faster than I did, but that doesn't mean I didn't drive here fast. I drove here real fast. Over the speed limit. Over what my husband usually drives. Which is faster than what I usually drive. He would be proud of me right now. If he knew. God, there's so much I wish he knew. My mind races with everything Johnny is missing while he's out hunting.

The irony that I'm out hunting now, too, is

comforting. I wish he were here hunting with me. But he's taught me a thing or two, and I believe that I'll make him proud.

My stomach is sick from hunger because I didn't want to waste time pulling off the highway to find food, so all I've had since my yogurt is a breakfast bar that was stuffed into my purse months ago and a stick of gum that was in my glove box. I know my blood sugar is off. I feel that crazed feeling that overcomes me when it is.

I'm also more sore and stiffer than I've been in a long time. Driving for hours is not something I believed I would have been able to do, without my medicine on me especially, but a mother's desperation will take her further than she imagines. What I wouldn't give for an Oxy right now though. Unfortunately, I forgot them at home.

I pass this man's house, the one who calls himself Tom, slowly and for the third time.

Lilac's car isn't there and I'm not sure what that means. If that's a good thing or a bad thing. I'd feel a lot better if it was there. I expected it to be. I wanted it to be. I can't believe the best-case scenario my brain could come up with was her being in bed with him and me busting down the door and smacking them both upside the head. That's how far this has gone. That would be the best thing at this point. But she's not even here. She must be with him. He was the last person she messaged both online and on her phone.

It does concern me though, that she hasn't been online or on text since early this morning when she posted the picture on her social media and now it's nearing midnight. Midnight. What could they actually be doing?

My brain answers that question for me in flashes of pictures that make me wish I hadn't even thought of the question. I go back and forth from thinking this whole thing is going to be fairly innocent to thinking my daughter is in a shipping crate to another country somewhere.

My stomach audibly rumbles, and I wish it was earlier so I could find a drive thru. My hunger wants to rush me. My physical pain wants to rush me. Wants me to prove something fairly benign so we can move on to food. Make me act faster, get done with what I'm doing so I can finally feed myself. Get back home where I left my medications.

But I know I must move slowly. Johnny drilled that into my head, back in the days when we'd go hunting together. Every move a hunter makes must be slow. Deliberate.

I park the car around the block, slip my ID and a

credit card in my back pocket, because I never leave them behind, and decide to walk as if I'm out for a midnight stroll. I need to walk because I'm hunched over with stiffness and pain. I need to stretch it out. I limp through it. I wish I would have brought the dog now. It's too late to go back, but if I had her here with me, I'd look less suspicious.

Instead, I slide my hand into my cardigan and run my fingers over the raised branding on my arm as I walk. I let it remind me that I'm strong. That I've been to hell and back and made it out singing.

I won't be a bad mother. I won't let my love turn into a wonky scar that means nothing but failure.

As I get to Tom's side of the block, I cross the street. The neighbors' blinds are closed and the first house I scope out is the one across the street.

The neighbor's house is conveniently overgrown with shrubbery, which means two things. One, they don't look at their yard that often, and two, their attention to detail isn't on the better side of the scale, so it seems like the perfect place to hide. It's also home to a large tree in the front yard that shades the yard from random lights and creates a large swatch of dancing shadows for mine to blend into. The closest streetlight is two houses down, so I blend into those shadows easily.

After an hour I've noticed that the house to the left of Tom's has a night owl in it. Someone that is wandering the house from the living room beyond the front window with a large screen television, to a kitchen that's attached to the living room. All their windows are still open and occasionally the outline of the man inside wanders out of both the living room and the kitchen then returns a few minutes later. My assumption is he's using a bathroom.

The house behind me, whose front yard I'm squatting in, hasn't rustled with any light or person at all. Either nobody's home, or everyone's asleep. Nothing has happened at Tom's house either. No lights. No movement. No brush of the curtains or shadows beyond them.

The house to the right of Tom's has a teenager sitting at the glow of a computer screen and music drifting from an open window. The rest of her house is dark with a dim light on the lower level that hasn't changed or been shadowed.

There's a car in Tom's driveway. I wish it were Lilac's car. If it were Lilac's car I wouldn't hesitate to march right up to that door and pound on it. Embarrassing her with a lecture until her light cheeks reddened and then pull her by the ear into my car and get the hell out of here.

But her car is not here. I keep waiting for them to turn the corner with loud music blaring from her stereo and laughing as she stumbles out the driver side door. But it's a little after 1am now. And that still hasn't happened.

The voice in the back of my head taunts me as it reminds me that a missing girl has forty-eight hours to be found before chances of survival goes down. We've just passed the end of day two. I'm not sure what the hour she left my house was, but we have to be dancing around that forty-eight-hour mark now. We must be close. And my patience is waning. Pictures of this Tom guy driving my daughter's body off a bridge in her own car start flashing into my head.

After thirty more minutes pass and the night owl next door has stopped moving around, I decide it's now or never.

Moving from the shadows with confidence, like I was supposed to be there, I make my way to Tom's house and check over my shoulder as I exit the driveway to the side of the house and past the gate, into the backyard.

There are lights on from the side, so I peak in the closest window. It's a small kitchen with an orange glow, but nobody's inside. Through the kitchen I can see a very bachelor pad style living room. I gag at the memories I have of being in a room that looked like that. A man with only one thing on his mind. It can't be good that this man's house reminds me of Dane's house. The memories of that history and my trauma make me panic. It creeps down my spine and wraps around the goose bumps on my skin.

I can't believe my daughter is old enough to be interacting with characters like this. I should have seen this coming. I thought I had given her all the warnings. Prepared her for a world where boys like this, in men's bodies, act like psychotic children on power trips.

Nothing moves inside or outside, so I go on, making my way around the house to the back of the house. The sliding glass door comes into view, and I exhale in relief. They are the easiest to break in through. I learned that when I was a teenager, sneaking back into my mom's house to get things I'd forgotten, or realized I needed to survive on my own. I never realized how handy the things my trauma taught me would become someday. But now it's gratifying that someday is here. Knowing that all my brokenness would have a useful purpose. They say everything happens for a reason. I don't believe that. But I do believe that what doesn't kill you, makes you stronger.

Standing beside the slider I hold my breath and peak around the corner. Still nothing appears to be happening inside. And since Lilac's car isn't out front, it feels like further confirmation that they're out somewhere. Probably a bar that closes at three, with fake ID's. That's what I want to believe at this point. Best-case scenario, if I'm being honest. It's what I'm hoping for. But the skeptic in me believes something darker.

I slide the driver's license from my back pocket around in the slider until the lock pops and then wait to see if anyone noticed.

Nothing happens, so I slide it slowly open, just enough for me to slip in, take one last look at the houses around the back yard, and then slide inside.

Everything is quiet and the yellow light of the kitchen gives the house a sickening glow against these late hours. I decide the best plan of action is to do a sweep of the house to make sure I'm really alone before I investigate. Since it's perfectly possible Lilac just left after seeing this creep zone and is almost back home by now. Maybe he's out at a bar alone, drowning his sorrows from her rejection. Yes. I've come up with a new best-case scenario.

How funny that would be. Me, sneaking around here, while she slides into the comfort of our beautiful home. The thought calms me even as my skeptic mind tells me all the reasons that is unlikely.

I move against walls towards doorways, into each room.

In the living room my eyes land on two champagne glasses, one full, and one empty.

"Dammit, Lilac," I whisper under my breath.

I move along the wall towards the hallway, and something crunches beneath my shoe. An earring. I study it, but it's not Lilac's. She's very obsessive about only wearing her product. Always the saleswoman. *It's brand building* she says.

I pocket the earring and my brows pull together in a scorn. This stupid douche bag. Lilac could have anyone, and she chooses this?

Down the hallway I find an empty, dirty, bathroom. Past the bathroom are two closed doors.

My heart is racing because I know there's a chance this idiot is waiting behind one of them. Shit. Why did I leave my gun in the car?

*I'm not here to kill anybody,* I tell myself several times in my head. *I'm a vegetarian, I hate murder. I'm just rescuing my princess from a dirt bag.*

My pep talk along with a few deep breaths helps to slow my heartbeat.

I swing the first door open as fast as I can. The hinges make a *squee* noise. It's a bedroom with a bed that looks like a five-year-old made it. I roll my eyes at the grotesque attempt. But other than the bed and the dresser that's probably older than this man is, the room is empty.

I turn my head towards the second door and tiptoe close to it. I press my ear to thin plywood but hear nothing. My fingers grip the handle hard enough for my knuckles to turn white as I build courage and then I push.

Nothing happens. It's locked.

And then there's a noise. Muffled cries. I'd know the sound of muffled cries anywhere. I've watched enough stalker movies to know that sound.

My hyper-mom senses kick in and I don't think before I step back and kick the handle clean off the door. The next kick knocks in the door.

There's a girl, stripped naked, tied to a bed with a gag in her mouth. My heart sinks. My body won't move. It's not Lilac.

Samantha

I'm sneaking into this guy's house. There's no sign of him or Lilac. Don't judge me, I'm channeling you.

# Chapter Eighteen

**LILAC**

Night 2

*It's 3am and* Lilac can't sleep. Not that she hasn't slept. She's been laying here in the same spot, sleeping off and on, in the backseat of her car, ever since she left the barn this morning. Right through the entire day.

She's left Tom to wonder what will become of his life from here. Let him wonder how much of a psycho she really is. She's hoped that he's desperate and hungry and scared. But mostly she's been feeling an ache in her chest that won't explain itself. One that keeps her muscles heavy and unmoving. Her stomach feeling ill with desperation to undo and redo so many things.

She's been trying to reason with it. Trying to erase it. Convince it to leave. But it doesn't listen. She's been crying to the point where she gets exhausted and sleeps. Restlessly. Then she wakes up and remembers the situation she's in. The hostage she's tied in a barn a few feet from the car and then she remembers he's the reason for the ache in her chest. She cycles through confusion, sadness, anger, and then exhaustion again.

At 3am she's in the part of the cycle that's heavy hearted, but not yet to tears.

She's hungry but she's gone days without eating before. Somebody told her one time that a person can only focus on one pain at a time, so she welcomes hunger pains and invites them to erase all the others. It's not working. But she refuses to believe it's not helpful. Plus she doesn't want to get up.

She wonders if Joshua felt this bad when he hit depression. Because she's pretty sure that's what she must be feeling now. This has to be the bottom he's always talking about.

Nothing has ever felt so bad, and nothing ever will again, she's sure of this.

She lights another cigarette in the confines of her

car. The window beside her cracked enough that she can ash out of it. The pack is already half empty. Her throat burns and her car stinks and she's heavy with the acceptance of it because it's the way she feels inside.

Her lip aches and she wonders if it's getting infected. There is no way cigarettes are good for her lip if she wasn't even supposed to be eating hard food. The toxic chemicals in the cancer sticks are probably keeping her lip from healing. It'll probably give her some hideous scar to remember this nightmare by.

*Perfect*, she thinks, *people should be able to see the scars others leave on our hearts. They should know what they're facing. People will be able to see this on me. It will hint at what I've been through in honesty now.*

She stares at her phone in her right hand, scrolls with her thumb to the message that makes her heart hurt the most. Like a rock sitting on her chest.

**Lilac. If you come here, I'll give you everything I could possibly give you in one lifetime. Because you are all I want. So come to me.**

It's her third time reading that line. She's read through every message he's ever sent her. Three times. A tear falls from the corner of her eye and joins the others on her face that she hasn't bothered to wipe away. The sobbing part of the cycle is just around the corner.

She's having a hard time reconciling the lies with the truth. Her feelings with his, and how different those feelings must have been from each other.

She touches the words and zeroes her mind in on how they made her feel, those feelings stab her now in the heart. She thinks that she must be bleeding somewhere. On the inside. It's a battle in her head between her feelings and her sense of reason.

Her feelings betray her reason and tell her she would love him through anything. Even this. Why not? Nobody else ever made her feel the way he did. She had felt as if she would die for him. And now she feels dead.

How could she be so dumb? She's always thought she was smart. Smarter than everyone else. She can't tell if the ache in her chest is from losing the love of her life to reality, or from losing her identity to it. Maybe both.

Either way, they're both gone. The love of her life is a lie. And she's a dumb girl.

She drops the phone into her lap and picks up the lighter. Flicks it in her hand, watching the flame dance in front of her, she uses her other to bring the cigarette to her mouth. She breathes it in, hoping it's killing her, a little. Relishes in the burning painful sensation of her lip being assaulted further. And then breathes out the smoke in defiance of its murderous reputation. She has no idea what she wants. She just knows that she feels too much, and she can't make it stop.

The lighter gets hot in her hand and her thumb burns against the metal until she can't take it anymore. When she finally releases the flame, her thumb is red and raw.

**Lilac. If you come here, I'll give you everything I could possibly give you in one lifetime. Because you are all I want. So come to me.**

She reads the sentence again.

She loves him.

She flips the lighter back on.

He's a liar.

She inhales another drag of her cigarette.

She hates him.

She watches the flame dance.

The conflict of love and hate dance in her heart and it feels like the emotions are wearing blades for shoes. Slicing her every time they twist or pivot.

She reads the line again.

**Because you are all I want. So come to me.**

What was he going to do to her if she had drunk that champagne instead of him? Was he going to rape her? Kill her? Kidnap her? She has no idea. And the not knowing tortures her. Knowing how close she was to being fully vulnerable to this liar's violence. Knowing that even if she asked him now, the answer would be a lie.

She gets out of the car.

**So come to me.**

The dirt crunches beneath her feet. Her steps are hard and loud, she makes no attempt at being quiet. She's the only noise for miles at this time of night. It's the kind of darkness meant for moments like these. Where nothing is as it should be. Her sadness and anger fight for control of her brain with every step. Her emotions bubble like acid in her chest.

She stops at the door of the barn and questions herself once.

*Am I crazy?*

*No*, she decides.

Heat is in her cheeks as she storms through the barn door and stares down the center of the structure at Tom. His eyes are rimmed with red, and his face looks wild.

"Oh, Tom. Haven't you slept at all?"

"Dammit, Lilac! Let me the fuck out of here! I'm going to call the police! You can't get away with this."

She laughs and she knows she sounds psychotic when she does it. She doesn't even care. She's been crying all day long and she's sure her face is puffy and swollen and her eyes look just as bad as his.

Her laugh must frighten him because he stops yelling, stops fighting against his ropes.

When she stops laughing, she's closer to him. Her cigarette is burning down towards her fingertips and ash drops to the floor. Her lighter is still in her other hand.

Their eyes meet and his feel like they're looking all the way into her soul. Whatever fear was there, is gone.

She matches his hard gaze with her own, clenches her jaw, and tries to stare into his bones.

"You've been crying," he observes. His voice low and even.

"I have. Thank you for noticing."

"Look." Tom hangs his head in resignation, "I'm sorry, Lilac."

She stares at him. Her heart aching. He's the only one she's ever really wanted. And if she's being honest with herself, she's not used to not getting what she wants. She makes things happen. She's a get-things-done type of girl.

"Go on." She purses her lips tight enough the hollows bellow her cheekbones sink between her teeth.

"I fucked up. I really wanted to be with you. I was afraid you'd say no, and I just wanted you so bad. You're so hot and I didn't think someone like you would ever really want someone like me," he pauses to look back up at her, giving her pathetically desperate eyes, "I'm a bad boy, Lilac, forgive me and I'll make it up to you."

She steps closer to him. Close enough that the top of her breasts, exposed above her shirt, can feel his breath on their skin. Her fingers slide into his hair as she wraps her hand around his head. The lighter and the hair wrapped up in her hand. She takes another drag from the cigarette and then throws it on the floorboards of the barn and presses her lips to Tom's slowly exhaling into his mouth, leaving little room for the thin streams of smoke to escape between their lips. It hurts so bad pressing her lips hard against his, the infection in her lip vulnerable and sore. They're both a mess. Everything about them is a mess. His wrists are bleeding from rubbing against the ropes all day and his face is dirty and puffy. Hers is stained with makeup streaks from tears and puffy eyes. Neither of them has brushed their teeth and the foulness of the smoke that threatens to suffocate him does nothing to make it better.

The photos she's spent the last twenty or so hours browsing dance in her head, the messages, all of his pictures, all of his sweet words, all the photographs she'd sent to him, and she wonders if she's going mad because her heart races a little. She slides herself onto his lap and presses herself against him. She bites into his lower lip, and she pulls at his hair, but he's not fighting back. He doesn't seem scared. He's confident. So confident her heart will win. He thinks he's played the best card. The strongest card. The one he's been playing the whole time. The strings of her heart.

Samantha

**Shit, Johnny. This is bad.**

# Chapter Nineteen

## SAMANTHA

Night 2

*"I'm not here* to hurt you."

The girl on the bed is looking at me with terror on her face. I can't imagine what she's been through. She looks like a child. In my eyes at least. Similar in age to Lilac. To someone else, it seems they thought differently.

I run over to her and grab one of the handcuffs that have her secured to the bed. She's screaming through the gag and pulling at the cuffs, trying desperately to get away from both the cuffs and me.

"Shhh. Shhh." I look over my shoulder, starting to be afraid myself that someone is going to come in from somewhere.

"I'm not with him. I'm going to get you out of here."

Those words seem to calm her.

The problem is, I don't know how to get the cuffs off.

Instead, I go for the cloth, homemade gag, stuffed in her mouth and pull it out.

"Is there a key somewhere?"

"I don't know," she says, and this triggers tears to begin to fall down her cheeks. That means her terror is giving way to other emotions. One's that will at least let her cry. That's good, I think. She's calming down from hysteria. I can work with that. I pull at the blankets underneath her and wrap them around her body, trying to cover some of the nakedness, trying to give her some kind of comfort while I'm trying to figure out how to get her out of here.

"I'm going to go look for a key, ok?"

"No!" she cries, "Don't leave me here. Don't leave me."

"Oh God, honey, I will not. *Not*. Leave you here."

I reach over and smooth her hair out of her face and look directly into her eyes, letting her know I see her, letting her know that I know she's human, that she's a child, and nothing in my being could let me leave her. Because nothing could. I would kill anyone that tried right now to get between me and getting this girl out of here. The mother bear in me has been triggered.

More tears fall helplessly from the corners of her eyes, and she nods.

*I'll kill this motherfucker. Lord help me, because if I find this man, he's dead.*

I search the bedroom she's in, which is mostly bare, and then the bedroom across the hall which appears to be Tom's, as quickly as I can, and find nothing except for dirty clothes, less dirty clothes, pictures of naked women from magazines and weird cheap sex stuff that's been ordered from someplace on the internet, I'm sure. At this point I'm pretty fucking disgusted by this man and I'm grossed out every time I have to touch anything he owns, but a key could be hidden anywhere, so I dig through his underwear drawer, and use a t-shirt to check under a dirty vibrator. I continue to not find a key and my brain starts contemplating if there's another way to get that girl out of there without finding a key. I'm not coming up with a lot of reasonable answers.

I'm imagining finding a saw and sawing apart the bed, which seems even more unlikely than finding the key.

There's not a lot to search in the living room, except couch cushions that have clearly never been vacuumed, so I run to the kitchen and start pulling open kitchen drawers, faster than I can close them.

I smash my hip into one and let out an "oomph." My pain levels are escalating and I'm damn near crying myself. My fingers in my left-hand cramp and my face crumples as my other hand tries to rub it out.

And then I see it. A gift from God. I just know.

At the end of the countertop in the kitchen, beside the toaster. It's tucked away behind the champagne bottle that's still half full, with only a little orange and printed RX label showing. But even from here I recognize the second half of the word on the label.

*...codone.*

I grab the bottle with every ounce of desperation that an addict would have. I don't think I'm an addict. But in this moment, I'm not sure. I need a pain med. I need it. And this seems like a gift.

The label says they're for someone named Janet and yes, they're Oxycodone. I briefly question who Janet is to Tom, but it doesn't much matter to me right now. Maybe it's the girl in the back room. Maybe not. I push down and twist the top and let a round white pill, just like mine, drop into my palm, then pocket the rest of the bottle.

I place the pill on my tongue, greedily, gratefully, and swish it down.

The next drawer I open blurs in front of me. *That was fast*, I think.

It must be a really strong dose.

Finally, I've found the drawer where he keeps his keys. There are so many different keys. I finger each one and try to make sense of them. I'm having a hard time. My brain is struggling against this medication.

That's strange.

I decide to grab a handful and take them all back to the bedroom. I'm looking down at them in my hand as I cross into the living room. They're all… blurrrinng…

**Samantha**

...

# Chapter Twenty

**LILAC**

Night 2

*Lilac's fingers tighten* in Tom's hair, and she slides her mouth from his lips to his ear.

"If you think your games are still working on me, you have severely underestimated your opponent, Tom."

The words slide from her mouth in a whisper and as soon as they're out, her head is pounding and she's falling to the floor. The barn goes black for a minute, and she wants to cry from the pain that's shooting through her skull but she's too focused on regaining her power.

He head butted her and now he's laughing, but his laughs are fading along with the walls and floor around her. She tastes blood from her nose in her mouth and her last thought before she blacks out is, *that's what I get. Fucking got too close to the prey.*

# Chapter Twenty-One

## SAMANTHA

Day 3

*There's pounding,* I hear it, but my eyes don't open. I'm barely aware of the noise. I think it's a door, someone knocking. No, they're banging. My brain reaches but that's as far as it can go, questioning the noise. It's satisfied that I answered the question, and it lets go.

Now there's yelling. Somebody is yelling. It's

distant. The sound doesn't blend into words. I can't even open my eyes let alone piece together a language. But somebody is yelling. The sound is muffled. It must be the person at the front door. My brain releases again. Satisfied I've responded to the confusion.

There's a girl screaming. That's definitely a scream. A girl. Maybe it's a television. It's so loud, high pitched, piercing through the low tones of the banging.

I can't open my eyelids, but I feel the carpet under my face is rough, not soft like carpet should be. It's crisp like the stuff that's aged poorly and has been shampooed too many times. The smell is dirty, like the bottom of a shoe that's been worn for years and never washed.

My brain shuts down again. I can't make it stay awake. The world fades away into black. I'll never know who was at the door. And I never piece together that the girl in the back room is terrified I've left her. But her gag is gone and so I've given her the ability to scream. At least I did that.

I don't know how much later, but later enough that I'm waking again from pure darkness in my head.

A darkness that is so different from sleep that it feels like waking up from death. There were no dreams, no faint memories, it's like my brain has been erased of the time that ticked in between the last time I woke and now. I'm not heavy with sleep, I'm empty.

The sound of wood cracking and yelling and more screaming breaks through my temporary death and this time it startles me enough that my eyes fly open. The late heat and sunshine of afternoon is the first thing I register. It feels wrong. It's night, no it's day. Why is it so late in the day? When did it become day? Shouldn't the air feel like morning? Crisp and new? If I've been out long enough for the sun to come up?

But the air is heavy with heat as if the sun has been up for hours.

Something very wrong has happened to me.

The girl screaming finally registers as more than just a noise. It registers all the way down and twists in my chest with horror. It's the girl. The naked girl. The one I found terrified out of her mind and handcuffed to a bed in a house I don't belong. The one I was in the middle of saving. The one I told I would be right back, just before I... before I what? How did I get here on the floor?

Shit.

She's been waiting for me. How long have I been

laying on the floor. What have I done?

Men in police uniforms run over to me and help me up off the floor, while more men with guns run down the hallway in the direction of the screaming. Their uniforms are heavy with protection, and I feel vulnerable and scared. I can smell the metal on them.

That explains the noise that woke me, the pounding and the wood cracking, they busted down the door.

The screaming finally stops so they must have found the girl. I hope they don't think I put her there. My eyes are searching for something to land on, to grasp at, to calm my disorientation. The man who helped pull me off the floor and directed me to the couch is coming back from the kitchen with a glass of water. I'm afraid to drink it. My mind is still piecing together what has happened here. How I ended up blacked out on the living room floor.

A memory of the knocking bleeds into my consciousness. Someone must have heard the girl screaming and called the police after I didn't answer the door when they knocked.

But why? Why was I on the floor. My blood sugar? No. That's dumb. I don't have blood sugar issues that badly. Yes, I'd gone a long time without eating much, but I wouldn't have just passed out like that.

Would I have? I had taken an Oxy. That's normal for me. Have I been taking too much? That doesn't make sense. Was it a stronger prescription than mine? It could have been. My brain grapples with the facts. It feels weak and like nothing is making sense.

"What happened here?" the officer with kind eyes and a dimple in his chin asks me as he kneels in front of me, coming down to my height and looking me in the eyes.

"I… I don't know."

For some reason my cheeks are wet and so my hand touches them. There are tears on my cheeks and it alerts me to my emotional predicament. I'm overwhelmed. I'm reaching through my brain to pick up the pieces, but not all the pieces are there.

Lilac. I came for Lilac.

"I was trying to save her," I mumble.

"We know, the police officer says softly putting his hand on my knee. I found the keys on the ground beside you. Someone is using them to free her right now. Who is she?"

I look at him blankly. He's not talking about Lilac. He's talking about the other girl. I don't even know who she is.

Where is Lilac? What happened to Tom and my daughter? Did they ever come back? How long has it been? Questions tumble through my head as I search the spaces up there for the best-case scenario. Because that's what I need. Worst-case scenario is too dangerous for me to think about now.

Maybe when Tom and Lilac came back to the house, they saw it surrounded by flashing lights and men with badges and left.

I want to throw up. The twist in my stomach is real and I fight back a gag.

"Lilac," I whisper because it's all I can say. But I say it so softly I can see he doesn't really hear me. He's looking at me and my mouth is moving but there's yelling everywhere, and my voice is floating into it, quieter than everyone else's and nobody hears a thing I'm saying. My voice sounds tiny and scared.

"The girl is naked, get her a blanket. Get her the kit clothes from my trunk."

"We used those yesterday."

"I have a kit in my car."

"I need keys!"

"I've got keys."

Nobody is talking about Lilac. She's not here. There's no sign of her. I feel alone, even as the officer with kind eye touches my knee and nods his head like he knows I'm struggling, but he doesn't understand. All that effort to be quiet. To not be seen. And for what?

This. Dammit. I fucked up.

Instead of saving Lilac, I probably sent that monster running with her.

"I'm sorry, I couldn't hear you. What did you say her name was?" The officer leans in and I can smell his masculine aftershave.

"Tiffany." A female officer answers him for me, the girl that was handcuffed to the bed is now beside her.

She runs to me and throws her arms around my neck bursting into sobs that unleash more tears from me.

The new officer turns to the man that's been trying to talk to me, he stands to greet her. She explains to him that Tiffany is my niece. She tells him that I came to rescue Tiffany and then never made it back to the room.

This must be what the girl in my arms has told this woman. Why would she lie about who I am?

"The only thing I can't understand, is why were you laying on the floor when we broke down the door?"

I make eye contact with her hard brown eyes swimming with confusion and suspicion. Unlike the first officer, they don't seem particularly kind.

I flash back to my steps before blacking out on the floor. I found the keys. I was walking to the room.

I took that Oxy.

Shit. It wasn't Oxy I finally realize. I'm such an idiot. I can't believe I took a drug from a pill bottle that wasn't mine.

"I passed out."

I don't want to tell her that I roofied myself, which I'm slowly piecing together is what happened. I know roofies look a lot like Oxy. I've shown pictures to my daughter online. I've warned her a hundred times.

"Low blood sugar." I add because I would rather like to avoid looking like a complete idiot. Even if I feel like one. Even if I know I am one, for putting something in my mouth and assuming it was what it said it was, even though it wasn't mine.

A third officer, a middle-aged blonde man with deep creases in his forehead, comes over and asks to speak with Tiffany. She wipes her face and nods while he leads her far enough away from the three of us that they're talking in private.

"So, you're Tiffany's aunt? How did you find her here?" The lady asks me.

"I uh, I... I followed the guy. Tom? He told her his name is Tom. He was taking her on a date, but I didn't trust him. When she didn't come out of his house with him, and I saw him leave, I broke in. But then, my blood sugar or something. I passed out."

"I have RA too," I throw in for good measure and extra excuses.

Wow. I'm kind of impressed with myself that I came up with that on the spot. I'm not usually a good liar. Johnny tells me that all the time. And it's true. It's why I don't lie. Usually. My face always betrays me. I can't see on these officer's faces if they see my face betraying me now. His face is younger than mine. Soft still with youth. But chiseled and sharp around the jaw with strength. Hers is older and more skeptical.

But Tiffany. If that's even her name. Has already woven me into a lie.

And I'm not going to let this girl down again. I already almost failed her once.

"So, what kind of charges do you want to file on him then? Looks like, kidnapping and rape to me."

I nod in agreement, because, like I know what we are supposed to do. This is their job. But I nod anyways.

"Sounds right. I don't think his name is Tom though. I tried to Google him. Nothing came up."

"Don't you worry about that. We'll figure it out. Let me get your number…"

The third officer that is speaking with Tiffany cuts him off as he walks towards us.

"Danny," he says in a serious tone that turns my stomach. I think he might know something of mine and

Tiffany's lies. I think, *if Tiffany is even her name.*

There's perspiration on his upper lip and his forehead. I hadn't even noticed that I was sweating too until now, when I see it on him. I wipe my own upper lip, self-conscious about it catching the light the way it catches the drops on him.

"We can't charge anyone with rape if the girl doesn't go to the hospital and get a rape kit. She's refusing to go." He looks at me. "Can you talk to her?"

"She's traumatized. She doesn't want anyone else touching her. Do you blame her?" My voice sounds accusatory, like it's all his fault that this is the process, but I know it's not. Not his fault. Nothing about the process of dealing with rape victims is sensitive to the victim. It's no wonder most rapists get away with their victims never even telling anyone. Who wants to keep the horror going when you can shut down and maybe put it behind you in some way? Reach for a future where you can block any memory of the incident. I don't blame a victim that doesn't come forward. I blame a system that is designed to keep them from wanting to come forward.

He takes a deep breath. Like what he's about to say isn't the outcome he wants.

"She has five days after her assault to go. Why don't you just take her home, and then make sure she gets in sometime over the next few days? Okay?"

I know why this isn't what he wants, I'm guessing it's because the more distance a victim can put between herself and an assault, the more likely she is to keep running from it. I doubt many victims go back to the hospital days later.

"I can do that," I'm nodding wildly, because in my head this all seems wild. Are things spinning out of control here, should I just make the girl go with them, with the ambulance here, am I really going to take this girl into my custody after lying to the police about who I am?

"Sure. Sure." Now I'm rambling.

*Stop rambling, Samantha.*

"Okay."

He waves the girl back over to me and this stiff, putrid colored, couch. I hate this couch and I want to get off it. I want to run out the front door of this house and leave Tom and his things behind. But I can't, I can't because this man has my daughter, and this girl is the only clue I have. And she's clinging to me. She needs me too.

She sits so close to me I can smell the odor of grease and dirt, like it's been ages since she's washed. I close my eyes and think I'm glad she's okay. Who knows what could have happened after I took that stupid pill.

What a stupid mistake.

I'm glad she's rescued. Even if this wasn't the way I planned it the first time I saw her there in the middle of the night. She's safe now.

"Tiffany," I say softly as I rub my hand down her back, my fingers catching in the tangles of her hair and moving out of them to continue to smooth her energy. Calm her down. Reassure her that she's safe now.

"Aunty, please take me home now, please. I want to get out of here!" There's still hysteria in her voice, her eyes are big as they plead with me to read between the lines, to recognize that she wants to run from this house as badly as I do. I know she won't feel safe until we've done that. Until she can breathe in without smelling this foul man and his foul house.

"Shh. Shhh. It's okay. I got you."

I wrap my arm around her shoulder and everything I say to her I mean. I've got this girl. I can tell she needs me. And I won't be letting her down. Every cell in my body that's programmed with the DNA of a mother knows that I will keep this girl safe from here on out.

I think she believes me because she starts to cry again. Her cries are hard and they're shaking her entire body, like a hurricane that's been holed up inside her waiting to break free. A release she's been too scared to allow until now.

"Come on," I say as I slide my hand into hers and raise us both up off the nasty cushions. "Let's get you out of here."

I make eye contact with the officer over the girl's shoulder, and he closes his eyes and nods. The girl and I turn to leave just as the officer tells me to hang on, he needs to get some information.

Again, everything I tell him is a lie.

**Samantha**

...

# Chapter Twenty-Two

**LILAC**

Night 2

*The smell of* something burning brings Lilac back from unconsciousness, her head is pounding with pain. The room seems to be spinning and she feels sick to her stomach. Vomit rises in her throat, and she swallows it back down.

Tom's face comes into focus and the tooth filled grin he's giving her sends chills down her spine and into the pit of her stomach. He doesn't look like her friend, and he doesn't look like he's afraid. He looks like he's in control. His smile and his face know, and they tell her, he's gained the upper hand.

Wait. Why is his face so low, so close to hers? She's on the ground. She looks around her slowly, the movement of her head making her nauseous all over again. This time she rolls onto her side and does vomit. She tries to bring sharpness back to her brain and her aching head. His hands were tied higher. Holding him up, he shouldn't be able to bring his face so low. His grin. God his grin is creepy. It makes her think, as she slides her hands underneath her and lifts her upper body from the ground, how did she ever find that grin attractive?

She turns her head and focuses on Tom and then she sees it, the smell that brought her back. It's the smell of his ropes burning away. At the same time the rope around his legs snaps, her memory of the lighter in her hand that ran through his hair flashes in her mind's eye. The tiny canister of lighter fluid and little metal fire starter, meant for her rebellious cancer sticks might actually be the death of her. The irony isn't lost on her as he lunges.

Her feet scrape the ground underneath her as she pushes herself backward, but she's not fast enough, he's on top of her. A splinter from the floor digs into the palm of her hand as his hot breath hits her face, his laugh deep and visceral. The look in his eyes is wild and savage. His hair hangs in his face as he licks his lips.

Her knee jerks hard upward. She drives it with every muscle in her abdomen, imagining it connecting with her own chin, but he's there and his groin is soft before her knee connects beyond his flesh to his bone. His face contorts and he falls to the side gripping his hands between his legs. She hopes he never has babies.

Her fingers claw at the ground as she rolls herself over and scrambles to her feet.

Tom recovers quickly and he's swifter at rising than her. Fear is penetrating every space between every cell in her body. Everything that was ever attractive about Tom has vanished and he is nothing but a wild beast at her back. The feeling of knowing he's bigger than her. Faster. Stronger. She's not the top of the food chain in this barn anymore. How naive she was to put herself here, in this position, alone with him.

His fist tightens around the strands of hair that fly behind her and her neck cracks as he jerks her body back into his chest.

"You fucking little bitch. I can't believe you thought you'd get away with this."

Lilac jabs him in the side with her left elbow and then her right, but his fist only tightens around her hair.

The pain is so fierce she swears he's tearing it out, and yet she stays connected to it, to him, to the pain.

"That's victim blaming, Tom. You started this fight." She forces the words out with spite, with rage, with anger that burns in her chest and never gives up. She doesn't give up. Her family doesn't give up. That's what they've taught her.

The side of his fist connects with the back of her head as he releases her hair and sends her flying to the ground.

"I was just trying to have a good time, sweetheart. You're the one who decided to play dirty."

This time Lilac doesn't acknowledge the pain that shoots through her body as she hits the floor, sliding against the rotting wood and riddling her hands with splinters. She rebounds like a cat that's been thrown, aware that she's in danger if she doesn't land on her feet. She's up in seconds before he throws himself on top of her and he stumbles over his miscalculation.

She takes the second that he stumbles, the moment of lost focus in his eyes, to connect her foot with his jaw in a roundhouse kick.

She sends Tom flying to the floor. She can see in his face that she wounded him. His hand coming up to his jaw in shock. She watches the shock on his face turn to rage. Feeding the flame inside of him that she lit last night when she didn't drink his drug. When she didn't follow the nicely laid plan he had for her. She'd lit a flame in him that has been slowly burning ever since. Her power like kindling in his chest. And now, in his eyes, she sees that it's out of control. Her fear is so primal it quiets every weakness that she should feel in her body. All she feels is the need to survive.

She knows now that she can't outrun him. Her instincts tell her to flee. But she's watched deer flee in her crosshairs and she's seen what becomes of them. Seen them fall, flying forward as the bullet slices into their flesh, the horror in their eyes when they realize they've lost their chance at survival. Her instincts aren't on her side.

Instead, she attacks.

Her foot connects again with his head as he's down on the ground, trying to get up. Smashes it back into the ground and it bounces like a basketball against the floorboards.

Her foot connects again with his stomach before he grabs her ankle and pulls her down on the ground with him.

She screams, but it's not the kind of scream a girl in fear lets out, that's not the scream that pulls itself out of her belly now, without her even thinking of letting it free. It's the kind a banshee screams to channel all the anger and fury inside, and she has so much anger and fury, it's the kind that lets its opponent know that it's not backing down. Droplets fly from her mouth and land on his face as they roll across the barn floor. Him on top of her, then her on top of him, and then him back on top of her.

She pins him for a second, but it doesn't last, and he rolls her back onto her back. His face is just as wild as hers with blood smeared across his cheek and in his hair. She imagines she looks just as crazed as him. There's no love here anymore. No lust. No pain that's rooted in heartbreak. There is only the pure drive of instinct that's born from two people with the will to survive. Both knowing that the chances of more than one of them making it out of this alive is slim. Probably none.

"Now we're having fun!" His words sound like snarls from a dog before it attacks. His face is that of a monster.

*He's not holding back* she thinks as he pulls his fist up high above his head.

When it connects with her face the barn disappears and so does the pain.

The world goes black, dark, timeless, and empty, for the second time tonight.

Samantha

...

# Chapter Twenty-Three

## SAMANTHA

Day 3

*In the safety* of my car, and a block away from Tom's house I turn to the girl I know nothing about, the one who I just lied to the police for and introduce myself. I speak softly so I don't spook her. I want her to know that she can trust me. That I'm a friend. I can see in the way that her hands clasp together in her lap, the way her eyes dart around the car, and the way she doesn't move to put on her seatbelt, that she doesn't know if she should trust anything or anybody at all. Which is a fair way to feel if you've been where she's been.

"Hi. I'm Samantha."

"Hi," she says. Quietly. In the same sort of soft voice that I've used with her. But she doesn't offer a name back. I don't want to push her.

It's terrible looking at her because her trauma is written in her every movement. Like a scared puppy who has run away from a life of abuse.

Trembling, she wants to trust, just enough to let someone help her, but the world has already taught her trust is too dangerous of an emotion.

I understand those feelings.

It took me a long time to trust Johnny after my mothers, fathers, and especially Dane. In some ways I still don't trust him. Poor Johnny. It's a hard thing to mend in totality. The ability to trust.

She's wearing a plain teal t-shirt and plain gray sweatpants, given to her by the police. I'm pretty sure she's younger than Lilac, which greatly concerns me. Not only because the man that has Lilac now, had her cuffed to a bed, but because she doesn't appear to have anyone that she wanted the police to call other than me.

It occurs to me that no matter how much she looks like a child, she's been through enough shit now to be broken inside.

I look at her a little longer. Waiting for her to say something, but she just stares out the front window that's covered in bugs splattered across the glass from the long drive here. I haven't had time for a car wash, but I wish she couldn't see them. I wish she knew I wouldn't have killed them if I could help it. I don't want her to see me that way. A murderer. Even if they're only bugs, I understand the way humans, victims in particular, can identify with other victims around them.

That's where Johnny and my struggles stem from. I've spent so long identifying with and as the victim.

But I don't think she's looking at the bugs. She's looking through them. Through the windshield. And through the world in front of her. I bet she's trying to understand all the big emotions trying to explain themselves inside of her. She's processing.

My eyes wander over the tan leather seats of my car, the fine wood grain on the steering wheel. I'm unsure where to go from here, but I know I need to start moving or her mind will start finding its way into the darkest places. The places she doesn't even know are there yet. But she will know. She'll find them alone at night. When she least expects to find them. In a moment when she finally feels safe or happy, her mind will find these places that are hidden from her now. The brain is gracious that way, it hides the darkest corners from view until we are strong enough to see them.

"Let's go get something to eat. You like fast food?"

She looks over at me and I see sadness and gratitude in her light eyes. She nods and I say *okay* slipping the car into drive.

The mother in me wants to encourage her to buckle up. Just whisper *seatbelt* softly, but the survivor in me knows she needs to not feel the constraints of anything right now. Including that woven piece of fabric across her chest.

The day I fled from Dane's house I didn't wear my seatbelt either. I shouldn't have even been driving. I only had my learner's permit. The flashbacks start to play through my mind as I'm driving this girl down the road in complete silence. I turn on the radio to try and drown them out, but it doesn't help, it never has. They come and go whenever they want.

Me working at Dane's self-owned auto shop, feeling so grown up behind the register when customers were there. It started with flattery. Dane always flattered me. Told me how pretty I was. How much I deserved in life. All the things he wanted to give me. Then one day he started saying he would give me those things. I ignored him because he was so much older than me and thought of it as him trying to be nice. I smell oil now;

it's not real, it's something my mind just does when these flashbacks start, plays tricks on me. We're lying under a car together in my mind because he needed to show me something. Teach me something. It's a tight space and I try to scoot away but he keeps scooting closer, his elbows brush my breasts and it's uncomfortable. But I don't say anything. He's my boss. I ignore it. I feel guilt about that now. Like it's my fault that I didn't do enough to stop him. The predator.

Things escalate from there until one day he tells me he needs me to help him bring supplies to the shop from his house. A house he shares with his wife. But his wife is on a camping trip with their children, so he needs my help.

I can see the house. I smell his breath.

I gag in the driver's side seat. The girl next to me looks over.

"I'm fine, sorry."

Sorry for my emotional trauma sneaking out just then is what I'm saying. What I'm apologizing for.

I shake my head. I can't go down this road right now. I can't get distracted. These are my dark spaces.

Right now, whatever this girl's story is, it's the only lead I have to finding Lilac, and that's what I need to focus on. Along with a solid, albeit fast, meal. A meal we both need.

It's not until I pull into a parking lot that she looks at me and tells me her name.

"Jordan." Her voice is soft, and her greasy blonde hair is in her face. She's trying to hide behind it. "My name is Jordan," she says with more clarification.

"Okay then, Jordan. Let's go inside and get some greasy burgers, french fries, and ice cream, huh?"

I don't tell her I'm only getting a salad because I don't eat burgers and I'm not going to tell her that. I'm going to sit down with this girl and eat whatever the hell she eats because she needs someone that makes her feel normal right now. I will be that for her. Even if it means I start drifting into my morally grey area.

She smiles with her lips closed, but it softens her eyes, and I know she's grateful that I didn't press her for more information. Or for more words out of her mouth. More than she was willing or capable of giving. We're both tired and hungry. She probably more so than myself. And I'm running on fumes. I haven't eaten since sometime yesterday. I'm so hungry I don't even feel bad that I'm about to eat a burger. My stomach may hurl everything everywhere when I'm done. A stomach does that when it's suddenly introduced to meat after a long time without it. I know because this won't be the first time I've cheated on my morals.

Once we've both inhaled a double cheeseburger each, scraped all the ketchup from the little paper cup with our fries, and are sitting across from each other with small white and chocolate swirled ice cream atop a small waffle printed wafer cone, that I ask her the big question. Well. One of the big questions.

"Jordan," I pause so she can register her thoughts, be prepared for what I'm about to ask, so that I'm not catching her off-guard. "What happened at Tom's house?"

It's an open-ended question without any assumptions. I specifically don't mention Lilac because I want to know if she will first. If she knows anything about her before I place the idea of Lilac inside her head.

Jordan takes a deep breath in while she looks down at the ice cream left in her cone. I don't know if she'll be able to answer right now. She is processing so much trauma. I wouldn't push her if I didn't need to, but I need to. I need to know as much as I can, so that I can find Lilac, and so I know what to expect when I do find her.

Jordan's face tells me what I already know, that it's going to be hard to put what happened to her into words.

"I'm a runaway," she says.

It must be the easiest part of her story because it's the first part she gets out. And she doesn't say it with her head down, but instead with her chin up. Which means that leaving her home, must have meant strength and redemption for her. That she probably had a good reason to run away.

"Tom convinced me to be brave enough to do it."

There. There's the first sign of pain. In the crease in her eyebrows. I see it happen in the shadow that crosses over her eyes. The way they darken.

"My mother got into meth a few years back, and I've watched it waste her away. I'm from Kentucky and in my small town I've seen it happening to a lot of people. Some parents are even giving it to their kids! My age! At least my mom never gave any to me. She was better than that."

There's a defensive tone in her voice as she protects what little integrity, she believes her mother deserves. I respect that, even if I don't agree with it. It's hard to betray your mother.

"A year ago, she brought home a boyfriend. He brought home her supply. He never left."

I nod and I hear it in her voice. The struggle to keep going.

Her sentences are getting shorter, and her mouth is getting tighter. Her story is getting harder for her to tell now.

"He started raping me eight months ago."

Jordan's eyes fall to the table and her voice is choked when she says it. She can't make eye contact and her face is red. She feels shame about what her mother's boyfriend did to her. Victims often take with them some of the blame. Even if they know logically it's not their fault. There's always a voice somewhere inside explaining that if they'd just done something differently, at some point, somewhere on the timeline, then none of it ever would have happened. I flashback again to Dane. I hate his face. I hate when I see it in my mind.

It's common knowledge that one in five women will be assaulted or raped in their lifetime. Jordan and I are both one in five. But right now, we are two in two. And one in five feels like an understatement. I think about the eight out of ten women, imagine them sitting in a room together somewhere, who think we're the overstatement. Who think it doesn't matter because it's not them. I question if these women are even real, or if the numbers have been inflated because women just don't come forward. I've heard they wonder these things about Jordan and me because they don't know any of these men who do these types of things. But can that even be true? I don't know.

I certainly don't know eight women.

My teeth grind together as I try to avoid thinking Lilac has joined our club now, too. Mine and Jordan's club.

"I'm sorry," I whisper. I put my hand out across the table to cover her smaller hand with mine. "Me, too," I say in the quietest voice I have. The gentle one that carries true sympathy. I wasn't raped by my mother's boyfriend specifically, but Jordan knows that's not what I mean by *me too*, both girls and women around the world understand that now. Especially the ones that have been through the kinds of things we have.

She looks up at me and the red in her cheeks soften, as well as the tightness in her lips, tears start to run down the side of her face and the rest comes out like a dam has been broken. Like she'd just been waiting for anyone to say those two simple little words. Someone to let her know she's not alone in her pain, her abuse, her undeserving guilt.

"I thought Tom was going to save me. I thought he was my guardian angel. He promised me that he'd take care of me. He even mailed me money in an envelope to take a bus to his house. The first night I was there he had sex with me. I told him no, but he just kept kissing me and pushing himself against me. I told him no so many times until finally I stopped saying no and then he did it. I was too polite. I didn't say no loud enough or hard enough. I didn't want him to stop liking me, I had so many feelings for him. I was so confused."

And there it is again. The guilt. The guilt that she must feel so that she can understand why the world would do this to her. Because surely it wouldn't do this to her if she was better. If she was smarter. If she had done all the right things.

The tears are coming harder, and her words are starting to be interrupted by gasps of air. I'm thankful the restaurant is empty and we are sitting in the back.

"Jordan, no. It's not your fault. Don't tell yourself that, it's not true. No means no, and every man knows that."

I hate the guilt as much as I hate Tom. Almost as much.

"I thought at least I liked him, you know. I thought I was his girlfriend, like I thought it was okay. He did it to me a lot after that. Kept doing it, day and night. More than my mom's boyfriend even. So much it hurt every time. I stopped saying no after the first time, and I just stayed because I thought he was the best I could ever have and he saved me, but I didn't want to do it. I never did. And then. Four days ago…"

She starts sobbing and can't finish her sentence.

Her hands cover her face and try to catch her tears. I'm horrified because it's not what I imagined. I imagined she was kidnapped or being sex trafficked. Something crazy, but instead, her story is familiar. A predator and a prey. A man saw she had no place to go, nobody to count on and love her. Like a wolf spots a lone sheep.

I think of my own mother who forced me to go work for Dane. Dane who saw I had nobody else looking after me.

This 'Tom' took this girl as his toy, and fed her lies of love, but she didn't even know what love was. And she is still a child. Fifteen years old maybe. The same age I was when Dane fed me his lies and then lured me into his den.

Too young. But too young is what these men prey on. They prey on the girls that haven't learned their strength yet.

I rise and go around the table to hold her. When I slide into her seat she falls against me, crying so hard it shakes my body, too. I wrap my arms around her and let her cry.

She doesn't need to tell me about the rest for me to figure out what happened. I don't push her to say anything else. I know what happened. I've been living it the last few days, too.

Four days ago, my daughter agreed to come see

Tom, just like Jordan did.

He hid Jordan where I found her. Naked and handcuffed to a bed.

I will kill Tom. If I ever find him. I will kill him.

Samantha

I love you.

Samantha

You know sometimes I still think about the people that hurt me. Purposely. Willfully. The pain never goes away. Randomly in the middle of a nice drive the pain will show up out of nowhere. For no reason. Even when I know all the answers and don't have any questions. I know that I just trusted bad people. The pain is just there. Stabbing me like the first time. I just want you to know. I'll never hurt you like that. I'm so glad that I know you'd never hurt me like that either. We have something beautiful.

Samantha

I found this girl that was hurt like that. I've got her with me. She needs us.

Samantha

Still looking for Lilac though.

Samantha

Don't worry. I'm going to find her, too.

# Chapter Twenty-Four

**LILAC**

Day 3

*Lilac wakes to* the smell of books. The same smell as the office in her house. For a second she thinks she's at home. That she's fallen asleep on the sofa and had a bad dream. Her head is pounding with pain though, and the awkward angle her arms are restrained at lets her know it wasn't a dream.

She's in a house on a bed. She can tell because it's soft like a mattress, and it feels as if a quilt is beneath her body, but she's not covered. She's cold and the sound of an air-conditioning that's blowing a draft across her body is coming from somewhere above her.

She can make out a big rectangular shape on the wall beside her that must be a bookshelf and the source of the reminiscent smell, but the room is dark. Very dark. If there's a window, it must be dressed in blackout curtains.

Her wrists are tied above her. Her legs, ankles, and feet are free, so she kicks around quietly, trying to reach anything with her toes. In the dark, the only thing she feels is the corner of a nightstand. She could push it, kick it over. Make a ruckus. She could even yell.

But she doesn't do any of these things.

She stays quiet.

She needs to think.

She needs to observe her surroundings more. Figure out where she is and why. What she really wants is for time to stop and let her free. To run back to her car, wherever it is now and throw it into drive, peel out down the highway and fly back into time. Back to the morning before her dad left to go hunting, and to curl into her own bed, under the blankets and wait for the sunrise. What she wants is to stay home from school and make pancakes with her mother. Her chest hurts with the desire. But that's not on the menu of options now so she's quiet.

She knows that Tom must have brought her here, wherever she is.

Tom is probably mad at her. Mad at her might be an understatement. The fact that she's still alive, alive enough to be tied to a bed, should seem like a blessing after what happened in the barn. She's seen enough horror movies though to know that being alive isn't always the blessing it may appear to be.

It's best if he doesn't know she's awake yet.

She holds her breath and listens.

Her face hurts where Tom knocked her out. There's a metallic taste in her mouth and her lip is crusted with dried blood. Her left eye feels swollen, and she's not sure if she is even seeing out of it. She tries to close it and she does, just a little. Enough to let her know that eye is still functional.

She wants to cry. She wants to call her mother. Tell her she's sorry. She imagines that she's lying in her own bed and her mother is just down the hall. That she could go to her and tell her about this horrible nightmare she's had.

She pictures picking up her phone and blocking Tom.

If only.

The floorboards creak somewhere outside of the

space she's in and her breath catches in her throat.

"Andrew! Have you taken care of that girl in my guest room yet?" An older female voice floats into the room around her. It's hard to make out the words but they come out harsh and angry yet distant.

*Who's Andrew?*

"Shut up, Ma, I'm going to take care of it. Just calm down."

Heavy footsteps pad closer to the door and Lilac's stomach drops. He's coming. Panic rushes up into her chest and she can't decide if she should scream for help or close her eyes and pretend to still be unconscious.

But then they move further away, they've just passed without coming in, his voice drifts behind him.

"I can't just kill her, she's famous!"

Lilac clenches her jaw and pulls on the tight cloth around her wrists. It's only cloth. She can get out of this.

*I can get out of this. I can get out of this.* She repeats the mantra in her head as she pulls and twists.

"Then why did you bring her here! You know I don't get involved in your girl problems!"

"There's cops at my house, Ma!!"

*Cops? That's good right?*

"Get her out of my house, Andrew!"

A door slams somewhere in the distance and Lilac

wonders who has just left. She wishes it was her.

Less than a minute later the bedroom door opens, it squeaks with a slowness that's alarming, and Lilac snaps her eyes closed and freezes. Even with her eyes closed the room is brighter. The light bounces off the back of her eyelids and her heart beats out of control.

The door closes again, and the light is gone. The room is quiet and after a minute she risks opening her eyes. Just a sliver between her upper lid and lower lid.

"Hey," a voice whispers beside her. "It's ok, he's out back. He's smoking."

The voice has a softness that reminds Lilac of home, of her mother. It doesn't sound the same as it did when it was yelling *Andrew*, yelling at him to get her out of this house.

She opens her eyes and looks up at the voice whispering beside her.

"Who are you?" Lilac whispers back at the woman standing above her, matching her voice level.

She's tall with curly brown hair and rail thin. So thin that Lilac's first thought is that she must have an eating disorder. If she was a little heavier, she'd say this woman could be her mother in another lifetime, if she believed in things like that, or if the same person could be in two places in the same world. Doppelgänger. That was a thing, wasn't it? Another person just like one

241

person in a different place. Maybe this was her mother's doppelgänger.

The same smooth light brown skin, the same kind, round brown eyes. She's at least fifteen years older than Lilac, but still, she seems too young to be Tom's mother. Maybe she was a teen mom.

"I'm Andrew's wife, Janet."

Wife?

The words echo in her head.

Andrew?

Who is Andrew? Why does he sound like Tom? Tom's dad? And why would Tom bring her to these people?

Nothing is making sense to her now.

"Who's Andrew? Where's Tom?"

"His name is Andrew, honey." The woman brushes her hand across Lilac's forehead with sympathy. Moving the piece of hair that Lilac always tucks behind her ear to the spot where she likes it, as if it's natural. Like she would know.

"He's a liar," she adds. In case it wasn't already obvious. "Pathological."

"Tom is Andrew?"

Janet nods.

"He's married," Lilac adds. As if it's something she can't believe, can't process, can't understand.

"Only because he won't give me a divorce."

Lilac can't decide if that adds insult to injury in this whole thing or not. She figures she's probably at rock bottom already.

**Samantha**

...

# Chapter Twenty-Five

## SAMANTHA

Day 3

*After Jordan soaks* my shirt with her tears for at least ten minutes, her gasps for air and sniffles slow down and eventually she wipes her face, and the tears stop falling. It takes her a couple of tries. She wipes and then she cries again. Wipes. Cries. But eventually she stops, and I place my hand on her back and say, "Hey, let's get out of here."

Once we're back out in the car, I'm emotionally

exhausted. I can't imagine how bad Jordan must feel. I feel stretched to my limit though. My daughter's missing, my husband's unreachable, I've got a girl in my car that I feel responsible for, and I'm running out of next plays. I don't know what to do.

I look over at Jordan and she's staring down at the sweatpants the police gave her. They don't really fit her. They're baggy around the waist and they're much too long. She looks as exhausted as I feel. Her hair still hangs in her face and the roots are slick with grease.

"Hey. I saw a Target and a motel on the way here. You feel like a shower and normal clothes?"

I figure she doesn't want to be walking around looking like an escaped rape victim with no place to go. Even if that's what she is in this moment. It's not all she is. It's not who she is. But I don't know if she can find who she is right now under all the weight of what she's been through. And I know the first way for her to find that person is to stop looking like what she is right now. A victim. She needs to search for herself in the simplest ways, first, before she starts digging any deeper. She needs to pick out her own clothes. She needs to clean and style her hair, and if she wants, which most survivors do want, cover her raw face in war paint, better known as makeup.

She looks at me and smiles. Her smile is tired but

it reaches her eyes and they say thank you, so I put the car in drive and head to the store. Feeling good that there's at least something for me to do, feeling a little less good about the fact that it has nothing to do with finding Lilac.

I think of calling the police again. But which police? The police here, in Utah, or the ones that told me Lilac ran away. And what would I even say? Hey, you were right. Lilac did run away, but I chased her, and now her and the guy she ran away to be with, are missing. I need you to find them both now because he's a pretty shitty dude.

No point in that. And the Utah police are already looking for Tom, with a fairly different version of my truth tied to it.

No, my next move is on me, whatever that is.

I slide the seatbelt across my chest and as it stretches across my lap it snags on a bump in the pocket of my jean jacket. I pull the bump out of the way and click the belt closed.

Then I remember the bump in my pocket is the bottle of pills. The bottle of pills that claimed to be painkillers and instead caused me to black out for a very long time. I had put them in my pocket at Tom's house. Before I blacked out. The pills were in a medicine bottle they didn't belong in.

247

My hand slides into the pocket and pulls them out slowly. Even seeing the bottle, knowing it's not what it says it is, makes me crave my own Oxy. It reminds me that I feel like I need them. I do have pain after all. And difficulty.

But there's something else in my head too, something new. It's telling me, maybe I have a problem. Maybe I'm abusing my pain medication. If I hadn't been so desperate, I would have never taken something from a prescription bottle without my name on it. That's asinine.

I really think I might have a problem.

Jordan looks at them then looks up at me. I look at the bottle and then look at her. It occurs to me that it might be helpful to find out where this bottle came from. I want to do that now. I want to forget about getting Jordan cleaned up and take up this new idea. Run with it at full speed. Finally. Something to latch onto that feels like something that may take me closer to Lilac. But looking back at Jordan, with the greasy strands in her face and the crisp victim outfit she's wearing, I decide that I can do both.

"Siri, give me directions to Target."

I drop the pill bottle into the cup holder between us before I begin following the directions coming from the speaker beside me.

248

"Don't take one of those," I say in a way that sounds like I'm joking. It's in poor humor though. It's also informative and honest. She just shrugs her shoulders like she would never even consider taking pills from someone else's pill bottle. Which makes sense. If a person were smart, that's the reaction they should have. And then I feel stupid all over again. It's fine though. It's totally fine. We all make mistakes, I tell myself in an effort to comfort my wounded pride.

"There's something I haven't told you," I say staring out the window and not looking over at Jordan. It's going to be hard for me to tell her that the reason her boyfriend handcuffed her to a bed was because of my daughter. I know from experience with friends that I went to school with, no matter how abusive a man is to a woman, if that woman identified that man as *boyfriend*, the feelings are complicated. And while it's pretty clear Tom didn't feel that way about Jordan, Jordan's a fifteen-year-old runaway that doesn't have a healthy relationship to contrast her abusive one with.

"My daughter," I start, "she went to see Tom. She'd been messaging with him too, just like you. As a matter of fact, Tom was messaging with hundreds of girls. I saw all the messages."

I look away from the road to glance at the girl in my passenger seat. Her head is hung, and she looks heartbroken, like I expected her to. She wasn't expecting more betrayal. She's too young to know that the depths of a betraying man's betrayal never end.

"That's why I was there last night. I'm looking for my daughter. She's missing. Her name's Lilac."

"She's a runaway, too?"

For the first time, Jordan looks at me suspiciously, like she doesn't know enough about me to trust me. For the first time, her intuition is making smart decisions.

"Not like you. She's sixteen and she was going to meet what she thought was the love of her life, but she wasn't planning on staying. She was just being rebellious. Wanted to do something wild and crazy. She's a bit like that. Wild and crazy."

"That piece of shit." Jordan starts to cry again. Her emotions flooding from her face as it turns red. She's putting the pieces together. Her pieces, plus Lilac's pieces.

"I fucking hate him. I hate him!" She hits the dash of my passenger seat, and I don't stop her, don't try to calm her down. She's earned this rage.

"I fucking hate him, too," I say in a calmer voice than her, but only because I have self-control that comes with age. I'm every bit as angry as her.

When we get to the Target parking lot, I park the

car near the front door, pull my purse from the backseat, and hand Jordan a hundred-dollar bill. Her eyes widen and her mouth drops open, then she looks back up at me without saying a word.

"Go get yourself whatever you want. Clothes, purse, hair ties, makeup, whatever, ok. I'm going to stay in the car and make some calls, do a little research."

"Thank you," she says in a voice that's childishly excited. The tone makes me smile and my heart breaks all at the same time. She's wiping her eyes. She's found something happier to focus on. It's the resilience inherent in the young. She's too young to have been through the things she's been through. But the world isn't fair, and the truth is, the young are the most vulnerable. Without someone protecting them. The hunters come.

My mind switches gears to Lilac. I guess they come even when they are protected.

Now it's my turn to hit the dash. Jordan has already disappeared through the front door, so she doesn't hear me yell *fuuuuuck*.

First, I call Johnny again. It goes straight to voicemail.

Then I call Tanya. Because I need to hear another adult's voice.

She picks up on the first ring.

"How's it going? You get your crazy runaway? You didn't kill anyone did you?"

She has no idea.

"No. I haven 't gotten her yet. She's not at Tom's house. Neither is Tom."

"Shit. Where do you think they are? Did they runaway together?"

"I really don't know, Tanya, but he's more than a player and manipulative little shit. He had a girl handcuffed to a bed in his house. She'd been there for a few days. She's with me now."

There's silence on the line. Tanya is stunned. I can't blame her; I wouldn't know what to say either. In the silence I watch an old lady push a cart down the middle of the road in the aisle across from the one I'm parked in. It's strange that no matter what kind of shit is happening in a person's life, part of the world still goes on like nothing is happening at all. The sight of her, the old woman, living life like she does every single day, makes me feel small. Insignificant.

"Oh my God, Sam, I'm so sorry. Did you call the police? Do you want me to come down there? What are you going to do?"

Her words are spilling out of her mouth now that she's found her voice.

"Yes, I talked to the police." I mean that's not a

lie. "And no, don't come down here. I need someone taking care of things there. I just needed to talk to someone. Johnny's still out of cell range."

"See! This is exactly why these *hunting trips* are bullshit. You always said what if something happens, and now look."

I laugh to myself despite my emotional baggage at the moment because it is what I've always said, but it's the least of my worries right now. But I'd prefer Tanya focuses on that rather than what I'm going to do. Because that's on a need-to-know basis, and I think it'd be best for both of us, if she didn't know.

"Well, if by some miracle he comes home early, please let me know the moment you see him, ok?"

"I will," she answers.

When Tanya's end of the line goes dead, I put down my phone and stare straight ahead. Jordan's coming out of the store, and I'm coming up with a plan.

What would my hunter say?

*Think like the prey.*

But what is Tom thinking? If he and Lilac had gone out to a bar and come home to his house swarming with cop cars he would have run. To where?

I look back in my cup holder at the bottle of pills as Jordan slides in.

Janet. Janet.

I pick it up and read the name on the bottle again. Janet Landerstrom.

A quick search leads me to a social media page with family pictures. A woman close to my age and two small kids.

She's pretty, the kind of pretty I know I am. She looks like me, light skin, and curly brown hair. Because she looks like me, I absentmindedly consider if we're related. It's something I've done hundreds of times, every time I see someone who looks anything like me. I imagine it's something most people do when they know nothing about their biological family. I ignore the feeling of familiarity and move on.

This is probably a dead end. He could have gotten this bottle from anywhere. But it's a start. Maybe she'll know who he is, a friend of a friend.

I keep scrolling.

It's a post from months earlier that makes me stop.

It's him.

It's Tom.

"Oh my God," I say without realizing I should have bit my tongue.

"What is it?" Jordan's looking over across the middle console now at my phone, too.

"He's married with kids."

Jordan's voice is small and hollow with shock when she adds to my observation.

"Twins."

The caption tells us both what neither of us says out loud. His name is Andrew.

Samantha

**Really missing you right now. Wish you were here. You'll be happy to know though that even though you're not here, you're still in my head!**

# Chapter Twenty-Six

**LILAC**

Day 3

"*He's out back*. Smoking. I'm going to get you out of here."

The strange feeling that comes with realizing Tom is married to this Janet lady doesn't have time to sit inside Lilac's chest by itself, because she's still tied to a bed and afraid for her life.

She pulls and struggles against the cloth that's knotted around her wrists.

"Stop pulling. You're making it tighter."

Janet's voice is soft like a whisper and her curls are in Lilac's face.

How could Tom, or Andrew it turns out, have this whole other life that he'd hidden from her? She thought she knew everything about him.

"He had his own house," she mumbles. Trying to piece together how she could have been so deceived.

"Well. Actually, it's my house. He has no credit. But I owned it before we got married, and then rented it out for a while when we both moved in here. He's been staying there off and on. We've been fighting a lot. I want a divorce. He's been cheating on me, but he thinks he owns me. And it turns out he's a liar. So. Yeah. I found that out, too."

She tugs hard at Lilac's arms, as if Lilac hadn't already tried that. As if she hadn't just told Lilac not to do that.

Lilac notices Janet's left cheek is darker than her right and even in the dark she can tell the under eye is bruised.

"He hits you?"

"Let's just say I'm in a little deeper than you," Janet says, and then seems to reconsider, "I mean, I'm not tied up, but I guess I'm kind of tied up. Maybe we're both in pretty deep at this moment."

She lets out a little laugh, like she made a sick joke that only someone with dark humor could appreciate. Lilac usually considers herself to have dark humor, but she's not laughing.

The hours she and Tom had spent sending messages back and forth, sometimes until the sun came up. The love, the adoration, the obsessing, it was all lies. Everything he'd sold her, the man of her dreams, her soul mate, it was a lie. He was a figment of his own imagination, and he shared that figment with her, and she'd fallen in love with it.

The magnitude of that lie is settling in her chest now, as this woman with a mark on her arm, like her mother's, and a bruise on her left cheek, is tugging at the tightly tied cloth around her wrists. Making little progress with it.

*Wait, why does she have a mark like my mother's? Didn't mom say that was a family brand?*

The cloth gives in the weakest way, but it's hope, hope for both of them, and Lilac twists and pulls, despite the orders not to pull. She's almost free.

Then a noise that sounds like a door slamming somewhere else in the house makes them freeze.

Janet brings her finger to her lips to signal Lilac to be silent.

Lilac's eyes go wide and her heart speeds again.

Panic is in her throat. She's still stuck to the bed, her wrists, and hands not yet free, but Janet has stopped tugging at the cloth.

She's standing up slowly and tiptoeing backwards toward the wall beside the bookshelf. She can almost hide behind it. She's so thin. But instead of stepping beside the bookshelf she bumps directly into it. The books shake, and some of them fall. The ones not supported by a bookend.

"Please," Lilac cries, "Just untie me, let me up."

The woman's eyebrows crease as her eyes widen and her finger flies back up to her mouth. Like she hadn't just made an obnoxious amount of noise acting like a scared cat in retreat.

Lilac whimpers as the door handle turns.

Sunlight floods the room as the door swings open. She hadn't been sure it was still day, but now she knows.

Andrew's eyes meet hers with hate and disdain, but it's quick. Too quick. Andrew's eyes are now more interested in his wife.

"Ma? Why are you in here?"

He is every bit the predator when he sees her, and it sends the hair on the back of Lilac's neck to a standstill. She should be more afraid for herself in this situation. Tied to the bed. The man she just kidnapped and left tied up in a barn, now free of his own restraints. But she is terrified for Janet because his eyes say predator and her body language says prey and Lilac has been raised to read that perfectly, so she knows. She knows what's going to go down. Maybe not the details. But she knows Janet's the one in immediate danger.

"Ma. I asked you a question."

His voice comes out hard and aggressive. Nothing like the carefree skater boy Lilac saw and dreamed of plastered all over his social media. The online version of him has morphed into something else entirely. Something manipulative, dangerous, and aggressive. Lilac can't even see the skater boy she thought she loved in him anymore. Everything about that boy was a lie.

"I was just checking on her."

Janet's voice is weak. Lilac observes this instantly. The weakness frightens Lilac even more. She knows where weakness leads. It's never pretty. Her stomach turns at the missteps of this woman she's never met before. This woman that reminds her of her mother.

Andrew speaks as he glides across the room in five long quick strides, "I don't need you to check on her!"

When he reaches Janet, his backhand connects with her face in one strong motion and Lilac gasps at the sound it makes. Janet flies into the wall like a rag doll. Not a muscle in her body fought back against the slap. She collapses into it like she's been there a hundred times and she knows there is no point in fighting it.

Lilac twists at the cloth, pulls desperately. It's only cloth, she has to be able to break it. She needs to help this woman. She needs to break free. She can't just lie here and watch this.

Andrew picks up his wife by the throat and pins her to the wall.

"If I need your help, I will tell you. Otherwise stay the fuck out of my business."

He drops her back to the ground and she cowers, covering her head with her arms.

Lilac knows that kind of weakness emboldens men like him, almost angers them, like a woman who's just been slapped and manhandled has no reason to act so scared, so she isn't surprised when she sees his foot cock back and then fly into Janet's thin body, but it still makes her stomach turn when she hears the bones crack and Janet's piercing scream of pain cut through the room.

"Ma!"

The sound of the cry comes into the room first, followed by a small girl that has cropped straight black hair. The same color as Lilac's. She's got concern and fear painted in the features of her face. Painted with wrinkles and shadows in her eyes.

She looks so much like Lilac that Lilac is momentarily stunned with a desire to protect this child she's never met, coming from her insides like instinct. Lilac yells out in a commanding voice that would suggest she wasn't in such a vulnerable position as Andrew starts walking towards the girl, all the rage still in his eyes.

"Don't you fucking hurt her, Tom. Leave her alone!"

Andrew turns his attention back to Lilac in amusement.

"Oh?"

He laughs at her and mocks her.

"Don't you fucking hurt her, Tom," he says in a high pitch voice that sounds nothing like hers at all.

"Haven't you figured it out yet, Lilac? My name's not Tom. It's Andrew. You've been catfished, you dumb bitch."

His foul language reminds Lilac of her mother strangely. She's always said that men like him use words like that to make women feel inferior. They have these kinds of words at their disposal and women know when they hear them it means they should feel bad about themselves. That's what her mother had said when she'd started letting Lilac use the word bitch without repercussion. Saying that girls needed to use the word, take it back, become desensitized to it. Lilac is so thankful now, because when Andrew says the word, Lilac feels her mother's strength in her bones. She feels a little less scared.

He steps closer to the bed and Lilac wants to retreat, to scoot away from him, but she knows she wouldn't get far because her hands are still tied, trying to move away from him would just excite him. She saw what he did to Janet.

"That, Lilac, is my daughter, Julia."

He steps closer and rests his hand on Lilac's leg. He wants her to be afraid. She won't let him see it.

"One of two, actually. They're the reason I was so infatuated with you."

He takes another step towards the head of the bed, letting his fingers slide up her leg.

"Famous Lilac from the internet. Your eyes, they look like Julia's eyes. Julia has her ma's eyes. And as beautiful as their ma is, she's a soft, dumb whore." He laughs as he says, "We're struggling in our relationship right now, as you can see."

Then he continues with a straight face, "I thought, you would be better. You seemed so smart and strong online."

He steps close enough to lean over her kneecap and sneer. She can smell his cigarette breath from here, but he's not quite close enough, the smell carries. She wants to spit but she resists. Waits. This isn't the time.

"But look at you now. You're no different from them. All of you girls. You're all the same. Weak."

One more step.

Now.

He is close enough now.

Lilac presses her feet into the bed, arches her back, and throws one leg over the other, connecting the top of her foot hard with his head. Perfect aim.

He falls back.

Julia screams in a high-pitched way that only a child can accomplish.

Another sound, a door crashing open, comes from somewhere outside of the room.

A second small loud scream that matches Julia's comes from somewhere else in the house.

Everyone's attention turns toward the bedroom door as a serious looking young girl, maybe fifteen years old, comes through it, following the sounds of Julia's scream. Long dirty blonde hair tied back in a ponytail and anger glowing in the lines of her face. No, not anger, rage.

"You…" her eyes lock on Andrew and his eyes

flash confusion.

"Jordan?"

Jordan runs straight at Andrew and launches herself at him screaming like a banshee, she must have a reason to hate him too, hate him as much as Lilac.

She scratches at his eyes and bites into his neck.

She's wild and fearless and for the first time today, Lilac sees something that pleases her. Really pleases her. She would laugh and cheer if she wasn't still tied to a bed, instead she takes this moment to again pull at the cloth that's loosening against her wrists.

The little girl, Julia, showing a fearlessness that's impressive to Lilac for such a small child, climbs onto the bed and then she's pulling at the cloth, too.

Finally, it's loose enough, Lilac's hands slip free and she's up launching herself at Andrew who has rolled on top of Jordan and just pinned her wild arms to the ground.

There's a strength in numbers.

A man, a strong man, may have the upper hand when he's fighting one woman. But Andrew has pissed off more than one. And now he is fucked.

For the third time today, her foot connects with his head. This time, blood sprays from his nose as his head turns to the side.

It streaks across his cheek and drips into his grin,

stains his white teeth. His eyes connect with hers and she smiles at him with the side of her lips, letting them turn up as she watches his grip release on the woman underneath him.

The moment he releases her, the girls' thumbs meet his eyes, and Lilac's other foot kicks him in the ribs. It's what he deserves.

Lilac is elated by his scream. It's visceral. Like an animal that's found its own place in the food chain isn't as high as it'd thought. Intoxicating.

"Lilac!" Lilac turns to see her mom standing in the doorway with a gun.

"Get that little girl out of here."

*Oh shit.* Julia is still on the bed, watching her father be beaten. The same way she'd seen him beat her mother. Who knows how many times? There is probably a lesson in that for her, Lilac decides as she picks the little girl up and walks toward the door, blood spray on her pants and feet.

"Hi, Mom," she kisses her on the cheek as she walks through the door beside her. She's the only person in the world Lilac wanted to see right now. She's the exact person in the world. Her mother's eyes never leave her target. Lilac doesn't expect them to, because if anyone knows her mother, it's Lilac.

She carries the girl down the hall where she finds

a living room and a second girl, one who looks just like herself and Julia, sitting on the couch crying.

"Let's go for a walk."

Lilac puts out her hand and the girl grabs it, happy to leave the house of horrors they had all been trapped in moments before.

The three girls with short black bobbed hair walk through a broken-down door and into a setting sun. One girl in Lilac's arms, the other holding her hand. The sky is painted pink and purple as they walk down the street, none of them saying a thing. They just head away.

They have all the trauma that comes with being girls in a world where a man has been stronger, meaner, and more willing to abuse.

But they don't feel defeated.

And they're right. They're not.

Because it's not over. Not for them.

"Look," says Julia as she points at a family of birds that take flight all at the same time from a tree beside them.

"Pretty," says Julia's sister.

Samantha

**I've got this, Johnny.**

# Chapter Twenty-Seven

## SAMANTHA

Day 3

*Everybody freeze* is what I yell, because the chaos in the room has escalated and there's blood everywhere and I don't want to hurt anyone. Anyone except Tom. Poor Tom thinks I'm going to give him the upper hand because Jordan takes her fingers out of his eye sockets and he willingly gets off of her.

Everybody has their hands in the air except Jordan. Jordan knows I'm not going to hurt her.

"Jordan, come here."

She starts to walk over to me, but right before she's out of Tom's reach he steps forward and grabs her hair, pulling her back and so I shoot. I don't give him time to use her as a shield. I don't give him time to start making demands. I just shoot. Because my aim is perfect. I spent years perfecting it.

I was a hunter after all. It turns out, I still am, I guess.

All this time arguing with my husband and look at me, we are the same, murderers. There's no cavern between us. We just have different motivators. And mine hadn't been triggered in so long that I'd forgotten.

I laugh to myself because I haven't changed at all. I'm still the same girl I've always been. The fact that I've been walking around our house acting like I've changed. All I needed was the right situation to present itself to show me, I haven't changed at all. I'm still the same girl my husband married.

I sigh with relief, looking at Tom laying there on the ground. A hole between his eyes, dripping with blood.

Jordan is staring at him too, her mouth hung open with shock. I'm glad she didn't have to be the one to kill him. Killing another human can traumatize a girl that young, even if he's done what that man's done to her. Now she doesn't have to blame herself for this, too.

I'm aware of the other woman in the room staring at me. I look up at her and meet her eyes, she's not even bothering to look down at Tom. Her hands are still up by her shoulders and her eyes are curious.

I feel like I'm looking in a mirror. She looks just like me. Even more than what I had noticed in the pictures. A younger me. A thinner me.

"You're the reason Andrew kidnapped that girl?"

She says it slowly with some confusion in her voice. But I'm not following.

"Me?! What the fuck does that mean?"

I'm still holding my gun, and I'm pointing it at her.

"He said he was obsessed with her because she looked like our kids, he thought she would be a better wife. It's because you look like me."

"It's not my fault. It's your fault. Why would you marry this man?"

There's aggression in my voice and I don't like her accusations. Her face is going hard, too.

"*Stop!*" Jordan yells. She's still staring down at the body.

"It's his fault." She points at the lifeless man. "It's all his fault. All of it," she says again, and I watch as tears form in her eyes and her face wrinkles with emotion.

She's right. Why are we, two women that don't even know each other, standing here trying to sort out our blame and deflect on each other? Why?

My arm drops to my side, I click the safety back on the gun, and then drop it. My arms are around Jordan as we both sink to the ground, in a pool of Tom's blood.

I rest my head on her head, close my eyes, and just let her cry. Because I can't make anything better. Even if I made it stop. I can't fix what's already been done.

A soft hand touches my shoulder as the other woman, Janet I assume, sinks down beside us and wraps her arms into the embrace. She's warm and gentle. I open my eyes to look at her, closer this time. Her eyes are like mine. Like Lilac's. I do see what Tom saw. What drove him to his obsession. His idea of destiny I suppose. It's funny and strange how little things can make us think other things are meant to be.

My gaze drifts down to her arm, without even really knowing why, but I know when I see it, why I did it. The scar. The scar that looks just like mine. Stretched and morphed because of growth that comes with time.

Janet.

I say her name again as I realize it's familiar to me.

It's what I knew but didn't want to believe the first time I saw her on the internet.

Tom, or Andrew as it turns out, brought me to the one person I'd never looked too hard for, but always wondered if I should. My sister. Maybe there was destiny here after all.

I look down at the body and the blood that's starting to dry, destiny or not, this man invited in his own fucking karma when he found my daughter.

I look back at the woman with her arms wrapped around both Jordan and I, in her eyes, and I laugh. It's not loud or hysterical. It's just a breath of humor really. I killed my sister's abusive husband. Life is fucking weird.

"We need to get the bleach," I say, in lieu of all the things I'm thinking. There's shit that needs to be cleaned up.

Samantha

**I'm sorry I'm always giving you such a hard time.**

# Chapter Twenty-Eight

**LILAC**

*Leaving Utah* is a strange thing for Lilac. She arrived alone, thinking she was meeting the love of her life for the first time. She wanted it to be the perfect story, one they would tell friends at parties one day.

Instead, she's following her mother and a girl she's never met before with Tom in her mother's trunk. She's leaving behind her a family she never knew she had. Tom's family. Which is a little too strange for her to fully wrap her head around.

She's learned some things though. She learned that adventures don't always turn out the way they were planned. She's also learned that her mother has the heart of a lion and that she's ready to fight for her. And to rescue her if needed.

She used to think of her mother as weak, and she sees that was a mistake now. Her mother is savage. Lilac assumes that must be where she got it from.

Samantha

Found Lilac. I'm coming to see you babe;
I'm bringing you a present.

Samantha

I think I solved our problem. The one we're
always fighting about. You know, you being a
murderer, while I'm a changed woman. God, I've
solved so many problems this week.

Samantha

I can't wait to get there and tell you all about
it.

Samantha

I hope the cabin has still got that shovel.

# Chapter Twenty-Nine

## SAMANTHA

*Johnny stands beside* me with his arm around my waist, a shovel in his other hand. My t-shirt is covered in sweat and dirt and my hair is filthy, pulled up in a ponytail at the top of my head.

I rest my head against his chest, and I shiver as a cool breeze blows across my flushed body.

Johnny kisses the top of my head.

"You okay? You need me to get you a pain pill?"

We've been taking turns digging a hole, and then covering Andrew's body. Johnny has done more of the work than me, but I think I did pretty well, considering I haven't had an Oxy in days. I don't plan on it either. I have will and strength that I didn't even remember existed inside of me.

"No," I say, "I'm done with those."

We stand there in silence. The kind of silence that married people don't mind. Both of us looking down at the two graves in front of us.

One old, one new. One my trauma, one Lilac's trauma. And Jordan's as well.

Dane and Andrew deserve each other.

I wonder if Johnny is thinking of our first real hunting trip together. The one where I got my first kill. I look up into his eyes, my best friend, my lover. It was his idea to go after Dane, back then, when he'd heard of what he'd done to me. He looks down at me, and smiles.

"I love you," I say to him with all my heart in my voice.

"I love you, too."

This family cabin, completely off grid, really isn't that bad of a thing I suppose. We should all come out here together more often.

## Samantha's diary:

*I did it.*

*I killed Tom.*

*Or Andrew, as it turns out his name actually was.*

*I say was because well, he's dead now.*

*It was a mess.*

*There was blood everywhere, but I didn't clean it up by myself. Jordan helped me.*

*She's a really lovely person and it breaks my heart that the world has been so cruel to her. I'm going to change all that. I'm going to make sure Jordan's mother lets me adopt her and give her everything she's ever wanted and more. I'm sure her mother will realize that in some space in her heart that she loves Jordan and she won't want to give her up. I'm sure because I'm a mother, too. But when someone's a meth addict it's pretty easy to "convince" them of things. And I can be pretty convincing.*

*I don't think anyone will miss Andrew. Or look for him too seriously.*

*I took my sister, as it turns out (isn't that the craziest story) to the hospital and we told the police that Andrew had fled after he'd beaten her. We'd pieced together for them that he was the man that had also handcuffed Jordan to the bed. Janet owned the house he'd been staying in. They're looking for him in Arizona and Southern California, where he was from.*

*Of course, they won't find him there.*

*I don't feel bad about it because I've done the world a service. This must be the way my husband feels after he's killed a deer. He's fed his family. I've protected our family.*

*Not only my family, but who knows how many others. I've done the thing that the police, and the law, and the courts would never do. I know this because I've seen what happens to these types of men in the system. They go in and then they come back out. The law doesn't protect women from these monsters. So I did.*

*I'd like to spend more time out at the cabin with a gun in my hand. I kind of miss it.*

*I bet Jordan will love hunting, too. Lilac hasn't been in so long, but she used to love it. I think I may start to love it again too; we'll see.*

*Maybe we'll go for Christmas.*

*Johnny's taking the news that we're adopting a second daughter well.*

*He's such a good man.*

*Jordan is going to fit in well with our family.*

*She's a very strong woman.*

*I think it'll be good for Lilac to have a sister.*

*And whoa, I have a sister! She stayed with our mother for*

*longer than I did, and she told me I didn't miss much, that I was lucky I got out early.*

*So now I have nieces, and Lilac has cousins, and we have each other, and Jordan has us, and Lilac and Jordan have each other.*

*And that makes me happy, because the thing about girls is, they are stronger together.*

THE END

## *Author's Note*

The first time I smoked a cigarette was after I was roofied by a man I thought I was in love with. I was in college, living in my own apartment, which is where it happened.

He and his friend came over to hang out and I trusted him completely. Because I thought I *loved* him. I was *following my heart*. Which was some very bad advice I got somewhere along the way. It turns out he was not trustworthy at all. And my heart was an idiot.

He brought a bottle of pills with him. He took

THE VEGETARIAN AND HER HUNTER

them out of his pocket and put them on my kitchen counter, said he was just leaving them there because he didn't want to carry them around in his pocket. I never imagined he would hurt me on purpose, so when he told me they were vitamins and good for your skin, I naively and stupidly believed him. When he gave me one to take, I trusted him. Because why would my boyfriend roofie me?

The next thing I remember is waking up on my living room floor with my dog licking my face and a note on my kitchen counter, from my boyfriend, saying he thought it was best if we broke up. I threw the notebook across the kitchen at the wall and walked to the gas station to buy my very first pack of cigarettes. I felt like killing myself. Cigarettes were the closest I'd go to that.

That's the symbolism to my own life experience in Lilac and her first pack. Her need to keep smoking it.

I still don't know what that guy and his friend did to me. Sometimes, if I let it, my mind will wonder away with horrible ideas, and I'll work myself into a panic. Who knows what they did? I don't. And that's the thing about a drug that takes away your free will, your self-defenses, and your entire mind. It leaves you with so many questions that can never be answered.

Lilac has these same kinds of questions about

what Tom was planning to do. There's no way to know what his fetishes are, what he would have done without her consent. What he would have done with her after he was done playing out his fantasies on her comatose body.

Months later I finally talked to the guy who drugged me, and he pretended I had gotten drunk and called him my ex-boyfriend's name and that's why he broke up with me. I knew that was a lie, but it took me years to process the full truth of what happened that night. What I do know, and what I'll never know. How I lost complete control of my body to a man and his friend. Guys that I trusted.

The sad truth is these drugs are called date rape drugs for a reason. They hide in the pockets of men that women have opened themselves up to trust, whether it's just to take a drink from, or to go on a date with, or to invite them into their home or heart. And the traces of what those men do vanish with the memories and leave behind broken girls that never tell anybody until it's much, much, too late.

Partly because they can't process it, partly because they feel guilty, and partly because they wouldn't want to hurt those men as badly as they themselves were hurt. The women who are victims aren't usually prone to destroying lives. That feels like something they don't want to do; they'd rather just move on. Stuff it in a closet behind them. Until the names of those men are something indifferent and irrelevant in their own lives. It's far later when the woman realizes just how much destruction was done to her. The dark places in her mind the occurrence created for her.

This book stemmed from that experience to bring awareness to the problem of this blackout drug. This date rape drug. That men everywhere get away with using. Awareness to the fact that women aren't educated enough about it. Because the victims are silent and confused, and the men laugh and fist bump as they get away with it. And it's in more pockets than we'd like to believe.

I hope every girl that reads this book has more awareness after reading it, and if she ever finds herself waking up hours later for no apparent reason, she's quicker to reconcile and recovery than I was.

I hope she understands that she shouldn't feel shame and she shouldn't be afraid to tell someone, a friend or family member. It's not your fault.

But more than that, I hope every girl that reads this has enough awareness to protect herself better than I did, or better than Lilac did. Only because I don't want these things to happen. But don't let that confuse you. I know whose fault it is. It's always his. And if society wants to do better, we need to blame these men and stop them. Get these drugs off the streets and out of their pockets. Why is there no visible effort of that?

We need to talk about it. We talk about meth, about opioids, about weed even… all destructive drugs that hurt the user more than anyone else, but not a drug being used to victimize women?

No matter how aware we are, there are still ways around our awareness, we all make stupid careless decisions, but sometimes even the most careful person is victimized, so if this story hits closer to home, like it does for me. Just know you aren't alone. You aren't at fault. There's a whole shit ton of us out there. And women are stronger together.

I'm here with you.

PS. I did not use any names in this book of any real people. Everything and everyone is fictionalized and made up. If there are similarities to any person in real life it is completely coincidental. This is a work of fiction; what I've just told you here is simply inspiration. Any other questions about the book and inspiration can always be asked on one of my social media pages. Check out my website at AudreyDestinBooks.com

# Acknowledgements

Thank you, readers! I could not continue to find motivation as a writer without your love for my stories. Every single time I feel like giving up, one of you tells me how much you love something I've written, and my passion is renewed. It means the world to me.

This book is so much better than the last book I wrote for three reasons, my editors, Ellie J. Grey, Gail Delaney, and Beth Notari. I have loved working with you ladies, my book is so much better because of you.

When I wrote Moving Forward Optional, I was just beginning to dip my toes into the world of being an Indie author. By the time I released that book, I knew I found the world where I belonged, and I was proud of it. But working with you has really taken my journey in this occupation to a higher level. Thank you.

Thank you to all the author friends I've made along the way who have welcomed me into the world of being a published author, I love going through this life journey with colleagues like you. You are my absolute favorite people and I love everything you write, because I'm also an extremely avid reader.

Thank you to my husband who has shown me that men can be good and worth loving, even after everything I went through. I love you as much as Samantha loves Johnny.

Thank you to all my children for showing me how much a mother loves her children, so please don't get involved with anyone like Tom.

And finally, thank you to my teenage daughter, who is also included above, your strength inspires me every single day. I don't know if I was even capable of writing strong female characters until I met you. The strongest girl I know.

CPSIA information can be obtained
at www.ICGtesting.com
Printed in the USA
LVHW040546050122
707688LV00003B/14/J